THE DOLPHIN HEPTAD

Amelia Lionheart

3rd Edition – 2014

Amelia Lionheart
The Dolphin Heptad
978-0-9937493-3-9 Softcover
978- 0-9937493-4-6 ebook (mobi)
978-0-9937493-5-3 ebook (epub)

Printing
Minuteman Press (Calgary North), Alberta
Information and Sales: info@mmpresscgy.com
Printed & bound in Canada

The paper used in the publication of this book is from responsible forest
management sources.

Other titles in this series:
Peacock Feathers
An Elephant Never Forgets
Can Snow Leopards Roar?
The Humming Grizzly Bear Cubs

To,
Mia & Jasper, It
was lovely to
meet you. Have a
fun time in Australia &
enjoy the adventure,
Best wishes
for conservation!
Elisabeth
20 Oct. 2019

Website: http://www.jeacs.com

Dedicated to my mother,
with love and thanks for teaching me to become a
book-a-holic, and for passing on to me her love of
writing and the arts;
also to my special friends in Australia:–
the families Hartnett, Ough and Wolfe;
and
Sea World, Gold Coast, Australia

ACKNOWLEDGEMENTS

Once again, there are many people who have taken an interest in my books. In this third edition of *The Dolphin Heptad* I would like to thank the same wonderful people who extended to me their support, encouragement and advice with the publication of the first and second editions:

> Joanne Bennett, Mary Anna and Warren Harbeck, Michael Hartnett, Sue Hill, Grace and Hubert Howe, Kristine Parkinson, Lushanthi Perera, Varini Perera, Nihal Phillips, Robin Phillips, Benita Ridout, Darryl Ronchi.

With respect to this third edition, I wish to express my grateful thanks to:

> **Glenn Boyd,** for handling the printing of the books and production of all marketing materials in his consistently exceptional and efficient manner;
>
> **Michael Hartnett**, who continues to provide unfailing know-how, inspiration, and business advice;
>
> **Sarah Lawrence,** for her advice, support and dedication in bringing these new editions, and the new book, to publication;
>
> **Elaine Phillips**, my cheerful editor, who proofread this edition with her characteristic good humour;
>
> and last, but not least, **my family and many friends**, for their encouragement and support.

Finally, this page of acknowledgements would be incomplete if I did not mention that this book was inspired by my visit to **Sea World**, Gold Coast, Australia – I had the most amazing time there!

Thank you!

YOU
CAN MAKE A DIFFERENCE

You are UNIQUE! This means YOU have special gifts to help change the world. Talk to your parents about ways in which you can recycle or conserve at home. Ask the wonderful folk at zoos and conservations close to you how you can get involved in all kinds of fun and educational activities. Get your friends and neighbours involved. Look up websites for zoos and wildlife conservations, and check out what's going on around the world!

THEME SONG

Jun-ior Environ-menta-lists and Con-ser-vation-ists!

When we think about our world, all the animals and birds
Who are losing their homes day by day
If each person does their part, it will cheer up every heart
So let's take a stand and act without delay!

We've decided we will strive to keep birds and beasts alive
And to make CONSER-VA-TION our theme
We will talk to all our friends, try to help them understand
That our world must come awake and not just dream!

All the creatures that we love, from the ele-phant to dove,
Must be cared for and well protected, too
So all humans, young and old, have to speak up and be **bold**
Or we'll end up with an 'only human' zoo!

Where environment's concerned, in our studies we have learned
That composting at home can be a start
And recycling's very good, each and every person should
Be aware of how we all can do our part.

To the JEACs we belong, and we hope it won't be long
Till our peers and our friends all will say
They believe that con-ser-vation and environ-menta-lism
Is the only way to save our world today!

Will you come and join our band? Will you lend a helping hand?
Though it's serious, it can be great fun!
Tell your friends about it all, let them join up, big and small
And our fight against destruction will be won!

Jun-ior Environ-menta-lists and Con-ser-vation-ists!

ABOUT THE JEACs

The JEACs (*Junior Environmentalists and Conservationists*), a group created by *Amelia Lionheart* in the first book of her series, attempts to enlighten children – through the means of adventure stories – about conservation and environmental issues. The author is delighted that the JEACs, once only a figment of her imagination, have become a reality in recent years.

The JEACs firmly believe that some of the key factors in **saving our planet** are:

- Participation
- Awareness
- Co-operation
- Education

****

JEACs' MISSION STATEMENT AND GOALS

We are an international group of Junior Environmentalists and Conservationists who long to **save our planet** from destruction. We will work towards this by:

- educating ourselves on the importance and necessity:

  o of protecting *all wildlife* – especially endangered species – and the techniques used by conservation groups all over the world to reach this goal;

  o of preventing our *global environment* from further damage, and finding out how we can participate in this endeavour;

- creating awareness of these issues among our peers and by sharing knowledge with them, encouraging more volunteers to join our group;

- becoming members of zoos, conservations and environmental groups in our region, actively participating in events organized by them and, through donations and fundraising efforts, contributing towards their work.

Table of Contents

CHAPTER 1

Together Again

'Hurry up, Nimal. The girls' train arrives in 45 minutes and it takes us at least twenty to get to the station,' yelled Rohan, banging on the bathroom door.

'Okay, okay,' came a muffled voice. The door opened and Nimal came out, rubbing his head vigorously with a towel. 'Calm down, yaar – you know I only take five minutes to dress after my shower.'

As Nimal dressed, Rohan picked up the telephone in their room and called the reception desk downstairs.

'Good morning! Please could you arrange for a cab to take us to the train station in fifteen minutes? Thanks a ton!'

He hung up and grinned as Nimal said, 'Boy, aren't *we* all posh and grown up, staying in hotels, calling the reception desk and being so polite? We're moving up in the world, old man, we're moving up.'

'Well, *you* certainly are,' said Rohan with a laugh. 'You've grown two inches in six months, yaar, and everyone'll be shocked when they see you!'

'Thank goodness,' said Nimal, tying his shoe laces. 'I thought I was stuck for ever at five foot five and would always have to look up to you.'

'You still have to, so don't get cheeky,' said Rohan, who was five foot nine and a half inches tall. 'Come on, yaar – you look handsome enough to impress a gorilla!' he continued with a chuckle, as Nimal tried to flatten his crew cut.

Nimal grimaced at his cousin as they left the room, went down to the lobby and climbed into the waiting cab. Having given the driver instructions in Urdu, the boys sat back and relaxed.

Rohan and Nimal went to a boarding school for boys – which they loved – and studies, athletics, numerous sports and karate classes kept them busy. Rohan was excellent at karate and was already a purple belt. He also enjoyed waterskiing.

His cousin, Nimal – their fathers were brothers – had grown up with Rohan's family since his own parents travelled a great deal. A year younger than Rohan, Nimal had a happy-go-lucky nature and loved playing practical jokes. He had a good brain, and in the last term, he had turned over a new leaf and was actually putting more time into his studies. He knew that he had to be disciplined if he wanted to pursue higher education and become a conservationist like Rohan's father. He, too, loved karate, and was a blue belt.

The boys were in exuberant spirits. It was the first day of their winter holidays and they were glad to be let off hard work. The previous night they had checked into the 'Shah Jehan Hotel' – a large hotel, located in the same city as their school – and Rohan's sisters were joining them this morning.

Anu and Gina went to a boarding school for girls, in the town of Minar, a two-hour train ride away, and the four children were a closely-knit group.

The cab stopped at the station and Rohan paid the driver, who thanked him profusely when he saw the exceptionally large tip.

'He now believes in miracles!' grinned Nimal as they walked into the station. 'There's Bindu!'

They waved to the porter who was their special friend. He always saw the boys on and off the train and knew the girls as well.

'I'll be there when your sisters arrive,' called Bindu.

The boys nodded and sat down on a bench.

'Ten minutes before the train comes,' said Rohan. 'Feels like ages since we picked them up in September to celebrate Gina's ninth birthday, and, also, to say goodbye to Mike before he left for Australia.'

'Yeah, that was fun – though I hated the thought of Mike going so far away. At least his flight took off from the airport here, so we were able to spend a little time with him.'

Binjara, the city where the boys' school was located, had the closest international airport to the Patiyak Wildlife Conservation Centre, which was where the Patels lived, and Mike Carpenter, one of the staff at Patiyak, had recently emigrated to Australia. The children were very fond of Mike, and since Gina's birthday fell on a Saturday and Mike's flight was leaving on the following Monday, they were able to spend a lovely weekend together.

Mike and the girls had arrived on the Friday night and checked into the Shah Jehan Hotel. The other three children and Mike, with lots of telephone calls and email help from everyone, had organized a picnic birthday party for Gina.

Then, on the Sunday, the youngsters had planned a surprise party for Mike. Peter Collins, who had grown up with the Patels on the Conservation, and was Mike's best friend, also came to the party. Co-ordinating things with the younger folk, Peter had taken a couple of days off from his job with the Criminal Investigation Department, and had motored down to spend Sunday and Monday with them.

'And didn't Hunter have a blast!' said Rohan with a grin.

'That dog's incredible,' said Nimal. 'I'm so glad we can have him at school in the menagerie. I wonder how he's doing? I sure miss him.'

'Me, too, but we'll see him soon. I can't wait to hear what the girls will say when they hear of the plans. I bet they're "dying of curiosity", as Anu says.'

'Yeah, especially since it was sheer luck that Mum called us last week and gave us the details. Too bad she and Dad couldn't make it today,' said Nimal. 'I sometimes wish . . . oh, well,' he broke off. '*We* know the secret first and can bug the girls by keeping them in suspense!'

Rohan gave him a friendly punch. Their personalities were different enough so that they got along well and were good friends. However, Nimal missed his parents because they travelled a great deal. There were certainly disadvantages to having a father who was in constant demand.

Greg Patel, a renowned computer consultant, travelled extensively both in India and abroad. He was very absentminded about everyday things and so his wife, Jo, much as she hated not being with her son, travelled with her husband to keep him organized. Greg and Jo knew that Nimal was fortunate to be growing up with his cousins and it was the best environment they could give him under the circumstances. His schooling would have suffered if he had to move around with them.

Nimal loved living with his cousins, his Uncle Jim and Aunt Dilki, and would have been miserable if he had to live away from them – he had been with them since he was three years old. His parents lived with them at the Conservation when they were not living in hotels around the world.

The boys heard a loud whistle and rose from their seats as the train chuffed slowly into the station.

'Rohan! Nimal! We're here at last!' shrieked a little girl, who was leaning out of a window and waving madly. Her masses of short, curly black hair bounced around her face, and her wide-awake hazel eyes shone with excitement.

'Hey, Gina,' yelled Nimal, as the boys ran up to the window. 'Where's Anu? Did you throw her out of the window?'

The train squealed to a halt with a grinding of brakes, and Anu, who had been hanging on to the excited little girl, poked her head out of the window, too, and grinned at the boys.

'Hi, Rohan and Nimal!' she said. '*Please* get this little hooligan out through the door. She's sure to topple out otherwise, and if she lands on her head we'll be in trouble.'

'It won't make any difference to her brain,' said Rohan, smiling broadly. 'She's already *non compos mentis!*'

'Oh – you've learned a new phrase, have you?' said Gina, grimacing at her brother. 'What does it mean and what language are you *trying* to speak?'

'It's Latin and means "not of sound mind" or, to be brief, *crazy*, kiddo – which is exactly what you are!' said Rohan affectionately.

'No, I'm not,' said Gina, who was quite used to the teasing and loved it. She gave the boys a high five each, and then withdrew to appear quickly at the door with Anu right behind her.

Rohan opened the door and Gina tumbled out into his arms. He gave her a big hug before putting her down and then she jumped on Nimal. Though tiny, she was strong and wiry; Nimal pretended to stagger as he hugged her.

Anu got out, too, and hugged the boys.

They were thrilled to be together again.

'Only Hunter's missing from our group,' said Anu. 'Where's he gone, and what's all the mystery about where *we're* going?'

'Hunter went last week,' said Rohan. 'Be patient,' he continued with a grin, 'we have lots to tell you.'

'After breakfast, please,' said Nimal with a groan. 'I'm ab-so-lute-ly sss . . .'

He stopped as the others yelled, '*Starving!*'

'You took the word right out of my mouth!' grinned Nimal.

Laughing, they turned to find Bindu behind them, with a large trolley.

'It's great to see all of you,' said Bindu, 'but how come you aren't going back home for the Christmas holidays?'

'Because our parents are sending us somewhere else – they'll join us just before Christmas,' explained Rohan.

The boys brought the girls' suitcases out of the train, Bindu placed them on the trolley, and they all moved towards the exit.

'So, where are you going?' asked Bindu. 'And where's Hunter? I miss his friendly bark and funny tricks.'

'He's been sent off ahead of us,' said Rohan, 'but the girls don't know where we're going yet, and we only heard about it a week ago. I promise we'll send you a postcard from there!'

'Ah,' said Bindu, winking conspiratorially at the boys, 'it's a secret for now, is it? Okay, you send me a postcard.'

'But *where are* we going?' begged Gina excitedly. 'Tell us soon, *please!*'

'Yes, or we'll die of curiosity,' said Anu, giving Nimal a friendly shove as he walked beside her.

'You'll know soon,' said Nimal. 'Boy, Anu! I'm miles taller than you now!'

'Good things come in little packages,' said Anu, elevating her nose, her straight black hair swinging in a ponytail. 'But I must say, you've shot up since I last saw you. Have you been on the rack again?'

'Now, now! No fighting,' said Bindu with a laugh, enjoying the friendly and affectionate badinage that always went on in the group.

'Gosh, I nearly forgot!' said Anu. 'Where's my knapsack? Ah, here it is,' she said, pulling it off the trolley and rifling through it. 'Bindu, this is for you from the five of us,' she continued, handing him a beautifully wrapped package with a card.

'Thanks very much,' he said, and as they looked at him expectantly, he stopped the trolley. 'First the card,' he said. He opened it and gave a shout of laughter.

Nimal, who sketched beautifully, had drawn a caricature of each child and Hunter, with speech bubbles coming out of their mouths, all saying 'thanks' and 'happy holidays'. Hunter's bubble had a paw mark in it. 'It's just great,' said Bindu. He turned to the gift next and removed the wrapping carefully.

'This is stunning!' he said, gazing at the framed picture. 'It's one of the tigers at your Conservation, isn't it?' When the kids nodded, he said, 'It's beautiful! Is this one of your pictures, Anu?'

'Yes,' squealed Gina excitedly, 'and when we were here in September, Rohan framed it, Nimal did the card, which we all signed, and then I wrapped it up, with Anu's help. We knew you loved the tigers best.'

Bindu was touched. He was very fond of them, refused to accept payment when he carried their bags, and would not let any of the other porters look after them. So the youngsters felt that they could show their appreciation by giving him something he liked – especially something they had made themselves.

Laughing and explaining they made their way out of the station where the suitcases were loaded into the boot of a cab.

Bindu shook hands with the children, thanking them again for their gift.

As the group piled into the cab, he said, 'Now don't forget to send me a postcard when you get to wherever it is that you're going!'

'We won't! We won't! Happy holidays and a wonderful New Year, Bindu! See you next year,' they shouted, waving to him.

'*Khidr*, sir?' asked the cab driver.

'Shah Jehan Hotel,' said Rohan.

Back at the hotel, the bellboy helped them with their baggage and they entered the lift.

'May I press the button, please?' asked Gina eagerly. 'Which floor?'

'Six,' said Nimal.

Gina pressed six, and within seconds the lift stopped at their floor. The girls had a room next to the boys and there was a connecting door between them.

The bellboy put the girls' luggage in their room, unlocked the connecting door and then left.

'Okay, shall we have breakfast now, before Nimal and Gina faint?' asked Rohan with a grin.

'Good idea,' said Anu. 'Gina's been complaining about starving ever since we left school, and I'm sure Nimal's been bugging you, too!'

Gina and Nimal ignored them. They washed their hands quickly and then went down the lift again, this time to the restaurant. They were all pretty hungry.

A friendly waitress seated them and handed out menus.

'I'm going to have my usual kind of breakfast,' said Nimal, scanning the menu hungrily. 'A lot of everything!'

'Mmmm! Smashing!' said Gina, with a sniff. 'Me, too! Bacon, egg bhujia, sausages, ham, toast, marmalade, jam, and anything else that's going – and, of course, lots of tomato chutney! Something smells divine!'

The others laughed and placed their order. The food arrived shortly and they tucked in.

Very little was said as they ate, other than 'pass the salt, please', or 'could I have some more chutney, thanks'. But when they had ordered a second round of food, they relaxed over it and caught up on news.

'Now,' said Anu, 'which of you horrors is going to tell us the secret of where we're going tomorrow, or is it that you don't know and Uncle Greg and Aunty Jo are going to tell us later on today?'

'*Well*,' began Rohan, who loved to make a mystery of things, 'Okay! First, the bad news – Uncle and Aunty can't make it after all. Uncle got a last-minute call from Holland and had to rush there to deal with an emergency. So, they called us and told us the plans – initially, they wanted it to be a complete surprise for all of us, but, obviously, they were stuck. They'll join us, with the APs, for Christmas, and they asked us to keep the secret and give you girls a nice surprise, which, being the wonderful brothers we are, we did!'

'That's too bad about Uncle and Aunty,' said Gina and Anu.

'I was really looking forward to seeing them again,' continued Anu, 'and I'm glad they can make it for Christmas at least. But, my exceedingly *wonderful* but verbose brother, we are still in the dark about where we're going!'

Rohan grinned at the girls, winked at Nimal, and said, 'Okay, what do you know?'

'We know we need passports; we know that Hunter was sent off last week; we know we're going somewhere warm, because Mum sent us summer clothes; and we also know that we'll all be together for Christmas – but that's it!' said Anu.

'Maybe we're going to have another adventure,' mumbled Gina indistinctly, through a mouthful of food. 'You know, like the case of the "Peacock Feathers" last summer hols at home. I know – we've become famous and Peter is sending us somewhere to solve a mystery!'

'Whoa, Gina!' said Nimal, 'you've taken on the wrong personality – it's *Anu* whose imagination runs away with her!' He yelped as Anu kicked him under the table.

'That *was* a fun adventure, wasn't it?' said Rohan.

They reminisced about their summer holidays for a while.

The Patiyak Wildlife Conservation Centre, located in northern India, was managed by Jim Patel, Rohan's father. Jim, his wife, Dilki, and the entire staff were passionate about conservation which included all species of animals and also the environment. Concerned that pollution and deforestation was causing extensive damage all over the world, they worked tirelessly to create awareness amongst the public about the dangers caused by this destruction.

Nimal's parents, and the youngsters, were also eager conservationists. In fact, over their summer holidays, the youngsters had started a group, and called themselves the *Junior Environmentalists and Conservationists* (or the JEACs for short).

'Now!' said Anu, rapping on the table with a knife. 'Coming back to the topic once more, where *are* we going this Christmas? If you don't tell us soon we'll beat you up!'

'In a hotel? Really, Anu,' ragged Nimal, sounding horrified. 'When *will* you grow up? You'll get us all thrown out and, after all, *we* have some dignity, even if you girls don't!' He moved his feet quickly out of Anu's range.

'Let's go back to our room and we'll fill you in,' said Rohan, continuing with a grin, '*if* you're very nice and polite to us.'

Anu grimaced at him and Nimal as they left the restaurant, but walked decorously to the lift. They went up to their rooms, Nimal stumbling only once on the carpet.

CHAPTER 2

Exciting News

Back in the rooms, before the boys could defend themselves, the girls grabbed pillows from the beds and pummelled them unmercifully.

Though bigger and stronger than the girls, the boys were taken by surprise and could not fight back normally, as when they were wrestling each other, so the girls managed to push them onto the beds and stand over them threateningly.

'If you don't tell us *right now*, we'll pour water over you,' said Anu, holding the glass of water she had grabbed from the bedside table over her brother's head.

'Pax, pax,' pleaded Rohan and Nimal, laughing so hard they could not have got up even if the girls were not standing over them. Gina was seated on Nimal's chest.

'Ooof! Gina, please get off me,' gasped Nimal. 'You weigh as much as a baby ephalunt.'

Peace restored, they sat on the carpet, and the girls glared expectantly at the boys.

'Right,' said Rohan. 'Now where shall I start? Hmmm – first a GK question – which is the largest island in the world?'

'Easy peasy,' said Gina immediately. 'Australia – of course!'

'Excellent,' said Rohan. 'Now, do you remember Mike Carpenter?'

'Of course we do,' said both girls indignantly.

'As if we'd forget him, dumbo!' said Anu. 'He's been in touch with us, too, and said that he'd met Uncle Jack and was hoping to get a job in a new conservation Uncle Jack was starting in Brisbane.'

'Where's Brisbane?' asked Gina.

'Eastern Australia – right on the coastline, north of Sydney,' said Nimal. 'Did you get another email from Mike a couple of weeks ago?'

'Yes,' said Anu, 'but it was very brief – just asking how we were and saying he was very busy but would catch up soon. That's it. Why? Is he okay?'

Concern sharpened her voice. Mike was one of them.

'Yeah, he's fine,' said Rohan, 'and tonight – or rather, early tomorrow morning – we're *going to join him and Uncle Jack!*'

'WHAT?' screamed the girls. 'You mean go to Australia? Tonight? Yippee!'

They did a crazy dance around the room, the boys joining in, and then collapsed back onto the carpet.

'Where are we going to stay?' asked Gina breathlessly. 'Will we stay with Mike and Uncle Jack?'

'That's the plan,' said Rohan, 'and, on top of that, according to the APs, we're not going there just to have a good time and live it up – we are going to learn about some creatures we don't know much about.'

'Which animals?' asked Anu eagerly.

'Sea creatures,' said Nimal. 'Uncle Jack's starting a conservation for them and will include whales, sharks, sea lions, seals and porpoises, to name a few, *plus* – guess what?' He paused, and the girls looked at him expectantly. 'Dolphins!' he concluded.

'Whoopie!' shrieked Gina. 'Nimal, that book your parents gave us had tons of information about dolphins. They're such happy creatures, with their smiley faces – they always seem to be laughing.'

'That's right,' said Anu, 'and when I read about them I wished that we could see them for real and learn more – and now my wish has come true. Wow, I can hardly believe it!'

'Oh, one more thing the APs said,' continued Rohan, 'was that we were to help Uncle Jack, Mike and the others. This is kind of a "busman's holiday" for us.'

'What?' said Gina, wrinkling her nose. 'We're not going by bus from here to Australia, are we?'

'No, of course not,' said Anu, smiling at her kindly. 'It's just a saying. When bus drivers take their holidays, sometimes they travel on a bus, so the only difference from their daily job is that they are not actually *driving* the bus.'

'Oh, I get it – thanks, Anu,' said Gina with a grin. 'I thought it was a bit difficult to get to Australia by bus!'

The others chuckled. Nine-year-old Gina was the youngest of the group and did not always understand her older siblings. However, they always took time to explain things to her and answer her questions, and she was never excluded from their activities.

'What are we supposed to help with?' asked Anu.

'Not sure, but Uncle Jack will brief us. What I *do* know is that they're just starting up and have a lot of fundraising and organizational stuff to do. We're to help with things as they come up. The APs, Uncle Jack and Mike thought that we would have a great time,' said Rohan.

'And the *Opening Day* will be a big fundraising event,' said Nimal.

'But there are usually lots of adults who deal with all that,' said Gina. 'Won't we just be butting in?'

'Of course there'll be adults – lots of staff and volunteers are involved,' said Rohan. 'But the four of us are used to working with the APs, and you know how many fiddly little things there are that need to be done – like running errands, stuffing envelopes, et cetera, and we'll help out as needed, without bugging them.'

'No mysteries to solve or crooks to catch, but a superfantabulous adventure! I'm longing to see the dolphins in particular,' said Nimal.

'Maybe we can swim with them,' said Gina. 'They're supposed to be very friendly.'

'Yeah,' agreed Rohan, 'and knowing Nimal, I bet they'll be trying to cuddle in his arms within seconds of seeing him!'

The others laughed. The special charisma that radiated from Nimal to all animals was incredible, and the others loved to watch him make friends with any creature within a matter of moments. Animals seemed to trust him instinctively.

'So why was Hunter sent before us?' asked Gina.

'Because of quarantine,' explained Nimal. 'If you take any animal to another country, you first have to get special permission. Once he gets there, he's kept in a veterinary hospital to make sure that he isn't bringing any diseases into the country. If he is passed as A-okay, then he's released.'

'But then, how come Canada wouldn't let Hunter in with his previous family?' asked Gina, remembering that Hunter had been left behind with the porter who worked at the train station in the city of Minar.

'Because, at that time, Canada did not allow animals from India – there was a scare about rabies,' said Nimal. 'However, they've opened their doors again, and there would be no problem for Hunter now.'

Gina's face fell at the thought of parting from their beloved dog. 'But . . . does that mean that they want Hunter back? I . . . I don't w-want to l-lose him.'

'Cheer up, kiddo – we're very lucky,' said Nimal, giving the little girl a hug. 'Rohan and I wrote to your station porter, Kishore, and asked him if the family wanted Hunter back. Fortunately for us, Kishore had heard from them a few days before our letter. Those kids missed Hunter so much that their parents got them a Golden Retriever pup, and they simply adore him.'

'And since Hunter is very happy with us and *we* adore *him*, they didn't ask that he be given back,' said Rohan.

The girls breathed a sigh of relief, and Rohan continued, 'We only got Kishore's reply two days ago.'

Hunter, who was just over a year old, had some quaint habits and picked up tricks very quickly. He adored the children.

Thoroughly excited, the group talked about their trip until the telephone rang. It was Jim Patel, and Rohan put his parents on speakerphone.

After checking that they had everything necessary for their trip, Mrs. Patel said that they would call the children at 10:30 p.m. to say goodbye, and that Nimal's parents would call them a little later.

'Try and get some sleep, children,' said Mrs. Patel. 'It's a long trip and, despite all the excitement, you'll be tired out.'

'Sure, Mum,' said Gina. 'I'll make sure they all sleep this afternoon.'

The others laughed, and she dodged as Rohan tried to tickle her. They said goodbye and rang off.

'Gosh, do you know what the time is?' exclaimed Anu, looking at her watch.

'Lunchtime, for sure,' said Nimal, rubbing his stomach. 'My tummy tells me so!'

'For once your tum's right,' said Anu. 'It's 12:30.'

They hurried down for a quick lunch of spicy Indian food and then returned to their rooms.

'Let's nap till 4:30 and then have a humongous tea. We could get room service,' suggested Rohan.

'But what about dinner?' chorused Nimal and Gina.

'That's why he mentioned a humongous tea,' said Anu, with a smile. 'We'll get food on the flights, and I'm sure the APs have asked for especially large meals for us!'

'The flight leaves at 2:30 a.m., Anu,' growled Nimal. 'You surely don't imagine I can survive without a meal from 4:30 in the afternoon, do you? And when I'm excited, I eat even more.'

'Well, perhaps we can get a meal at the airport once we've checked in,' said Rohan with a grin. 'After all, better to feed the brute, Anu, than have to carry a large heffalump like him around if he faints from hunger.'

He dodged as Nimal aimed a karate kick at him, grabbed his leg and threw him onto the carpet.

'Cool it, boys,' said Anu. 'You needn't show us how good you are at karate. We're starting classes, too, next term. What's the plan from now on, Rohan?'

'We leave here by cab at 11 p.m., arrive at the airport by 11:30, check in immediately, and I guess then we go to the boarding lounge and wait to get on the plane.'

'It's a Boeing 747,' said Nimal gleefully, 'a jumbo jet – the largest plane we've ever been on.'

'Which airline are we taking, and what's the route?' asked Anu.

'Singapore Airlines from here to Singapore – four hours and fifteen minutes, a three-hour stopover in Singapore, and then the Qantas flight to Brisbane, which is seven hours,' said Rohan, who had memorized their itinerary. 'We won't have to hang around much in Singapore,' he continued, 'because as soon as our flight lands we have to confirm our seats on the Qantas flight. Then we have to cash a traveller's cheque, buy a telephone card, and call the APs in India and Holland. We can pick up something nice from the duty free shops for Uncle Jack, Mike, and any others we meet, and after that, head straight to the boarding lounge. Our visas for Australia are stamped in our passports. We don't need visas for Singapore.'

'Did the APs send us some money?' asked Anu.

'Enough for emergencies and extra food,' said Rohan. 'Once we get to Brisbane, Dad has asked Mike and Uncle Jack to give us whatever we need, and they'll settle it among themselves.'

The youngsters chatted about Jack.

Jack Larkin, an Australian, was well known as a passionate conservationist. He had set up conservations in many cities in Australia, as well as one in New Zealand, and had been called in as a consultant to assist with setting them up in several other countries.

He and Jim Patel first met in India, many years before, at an international conference on conservation. They had hit it off immediately. Jim invited Jack to his home – Jack fit right in with the family, and the youngsters adored him. He visited India frequently, but the children did not see as much of him as they would have liked to, because his trips did not always coincide with their school breaks. However, they got news of him through their parents and via occasional emails from him.

Jack had no children of his own, but he had two nieces, his brother's children, whom he loved dearly. However, as they lived in Canada, he did not see them too often since he worked mainly in the eastern countries and all around Australia.

'Hey, it's nearly 1:30,' said Rohan, looking at his watch, 'time for a nap, folks! I'll set my alarm for 4:30.'

Despite their excitement about the trip to Australia, the girls, who had been up since four that morning, fell asleep quickly. The boys took a bit longer, but soon all four were dreaming about a wonderful trip 'down under'.

No one stirred until Rohan, whose alarm went off at 4:30, shook each of them awake.

They ordered a sumptuous tea and lazed around the table after the meal.

'Have you written any more poetry, Gina?' asked Nimal.

'Yes, I wrote one about the lovely birthday picnic you gave me.'

'Let's hear it, then!' said everyone.

The little girl had a talent for writing verse, and appeared to enjoy it very much indeed.

'It's called *A Superfantabulous Day!*' said Gina, and took a deep breath.

It was my birthday, I'd be nine, and luckily for me
It fell upon a Saturday, when all of us were free.
Mike was going far away, and though it made us sad,
He would be with us on my day, and we were really glad!

On Friday Mike picked up us gals, to meet the rest we went
We checked into a grand hotel, and there the night we spent
We woke up on my birthday, I'm such a lucky thing
'Cause everyone had planned the day, to make me laugh and sing!

Old Hunter, first, did wake me up – his kiss was very licky
I didn't have to wash my face, his tongue is wet and sticky!
Then everybody sang for me, before I got a call
Mum and Dad were first to ring, then uncles, aunts and all.

They would not tell me anything, not even drop a hint
They covered up my eyes, you know, with a large piece of lint
Then Anu led me by the hand, I couldn't see a thing
They put me in a motor car, and ordered me to sing.

I sang because I had no choice, I sang and they joined in
Then all at once the car wheels screeched and made an awful din!
They got me out, Mike picked me up and put me way up high
He sat me on his shoulders; if I stretched I'd touch the sky!

We seemed to go on endlessly, but then I touched the ground
They made me sit upon some grass, while they all bustled round
When finally they set me free and I could see once more
We were settled in a gorgeous park, a perfect place for sure!

They'd planned for me a treasure hunt, a feast and games and cake!

From home and from Australia, gifts, 'twas more than I could take
I had the most amazing day, we spent the whole day out
Songs and laughter, photos, too, great fun without a doubt.

I am so lucky, as you see, I had a superb day
I will be writing to you all, before I hit the hay!
Thank you all for loving me, for showing me you care
It means a lot to me, you see, my 'family' from everywhere!

There was a stunned silence, while her family who were present first gaped at her and then cheered loudly.

'You're getting really good, Gina,' said Anu. 'Did you send it to Mum and Dad?'

'Nope,' said Gina shyly, 'but I guess I could send it by email. Only, it'll have to wait till we get to Australia and I can use Uncle Jack's computer.'

'I'm positive there must be a computer in the hotel,' said Rohan. 'Let's check.'

He picked up the telephone and spoke to the receptionist, who told him that they certainly did have email facilities for guests at their Business Centre, and that he could come down and use a computer any time.

So they trooped down and hung about while Anu typed in the poem – she was quickest on the keyboard. Then they each added a short note and sent it off to their parents.

By the time they had finished it was nearly 7 p.m.

'What do you want to do now?' asked Rohan, when they were back in their rooms.

'I'm going to read,' said Anu immediately.

She was a voracious reader and never had enough time for her books during school term.

'I'll read, too – in bed,' said Nimal with a grin.

'What about you, Gina?' asked Rohan. The little girl was humming to herself. 'Gina?' he repeated a bit louder, when he got no response.

'Oh, sorry, Rohan,' said Gina, coming out of her reverie with a start. 'What did you say?'

'You're getting to be almost as spaced out as Anu when she's dreaming up her stories,' said Rohan with a grin.

Gina smiled apologetically and said, 'Actually, I was thinking of a new tune.'

Fortunately, since the boys had been forewarned by Anu that Gina was getting more and more into her music, they did not tease her. She often forgot everything else if she was listening to or playing her beloved music. She had started taking piano lessons and theory this term and the music teacher was amazed at how quickly she advanced. Gina already played the flute and recorder beautifully, but thinking up tunes was new to her siblings.

'Er . . . what kind of tune, Gina?' asked Rohan, not sure if she would be willing to talk about it.

'Well, it keeps jigging around in my head,' said Gina petulantly, 'but I can't seem to grab it. I don't have enough theory to write it down and it's bugging me!'

'What about playing it on your flute or recorder?' suggested Nimal, tentatively. 'You're able to play a tune over a few times and then you never seem to forget it.'

Gina stared at him, and then, hugging him impulsively as a thank you, she rushed over to her hand luggage and took out her flute. She settled into a corner of their bedroom and started playing softly to herself, totally oblivious of the others.

'That kid will be famous some day,' said Anu softly, looking at her little sister with love and pride. 'It's the third time she's spaced out with her music since October. I bet it won't be long before she's composing seriously. Just listen to that piece of music – isn't it beautiful?'

'It's like a rippling, bubbling stream,' said Nimal, closing his eyes and swaying to the music. 'I can just *see* the stream, if you know what I mean.'

'Yeah,' said Rohan slowly. 'We've got a budding genius in the family.'

The three older ones were very good at academic studies, while Gina just scraped through. Fortunately for her, the family believed that academics were not the be-all and end-all in life, and that becoming a well-rounded, caring, loving human being was far more important. The children were encouraged to use their individual talents, too.

Gina played her flute softly, mastered the tune and then went to bed. She was asleep by 7:30 while the others read for a while and then dozed off, too.

CHAPTER 3

Travelling Fun

Anu was up first. She checked the time and, seeing that it was only a quarter to ten, she switched on the bedside lamp, quietly packed the few things they had taken out during the day, and then sat by the window to dream about the trip. At ten past ten she woke Gina.

The little girl looked at her in surprise, wondering what Anu was doing in her dormitory at school, and then, remembering where they were going, she jumped out of bed.

'Gina, go and see if the boys are up,' said Anu.

'Okay, sis,' said Gina, and ran into the boys' room. 'They're up and ready, Anu,' she said, coming back to dress quickly.

They were very excited! This was the first time they were travelling abroad and on such a long trip, or flying on a jumbo jet. So far they had only been on short flights within India itself and were always accompanied by an adult.

At 10:30 p.m. the telephone rang in the boys' room where they had gathered.

'Right on the dot as usual,' said Rohan, picking it up.

Mr. and Mrs. Patel's voices came over the speakerphone, and the children chatted with them eagerly.

'You sound extremely wide awake, all of you,' said Mrs. Patel. 'Gina, thank you so much for sending us your latest poem – we read it earlier this evening.'

'Yes,' said her father, 'it was excellent. I hope you'll write some in Australia and send us copies.'

'You bet I will,' said Gina, who was bouncing about. 'I'll send you poems about kangaroos, koalas, dolphins, Uncle Jack, Mike, and anything else new!'

Everyone laughed, and after a few last-minute instructions, their parents said goodbye, reminded them to call from Singapore, and rang off.

A few minutes later the telephone rang again and this time it was Nimal's parents calling from Holland. After a brief chat, they, too, said goodbye, and that they would look forward to a call from Singapore.

'And, now,' said Rohan, 'it's five to eleven and we'd better get going.'

He called the reception desk and the bellboy came to help them. Within a few minutes, they had thanked the hotel staff and were safely in a cab and on their way.

They reached the airport just before 11:30, unloaded their luggage onto two trolleys, which the boys took over, and walked into the terminal.

'Right, let's deal with the baggage first,' said Rohan. 'Look out for the counter which says "Singapore Airlines SQ456".'

'There it is,' said Anu, 'the last one on our left.'

They moved over to the counter where a cheery-looking airlines officer was assisting passengers.

'Good evening, sir,' he said as Rohan approached the counter, the others right behind him.

'Hello,' said Rohan. 'We're all together and I have our tickets and passports. Can we check in now?'

'Sure thing,' said the officer cheerfully. 'And where are you going tonight?'

'Australia,' said Nimal.

'First time there?' asked the officer.

As the children nodded, he continued, 'Are you on your own? No parents?'

'The APs couldn't make it,' said Anu.

'APs?' asked the officer.

'Sorry – Aged Parents,' explained Anu with a chuckle.

'That's a good one – I must remember it,' laughed the officer. 'Well, you make sure you have a great time in Australia,' he said, 'and don't forget to say "G'day mate" to everyone you meet, including the kangaroos.'

They nodded since they had often heard Jack say 'G'day mate', and knew that this was one of the traditional Australian greetings.

'Now, please load the luggage onto the weighing scales, young man,' said the officer, turning to Nimal, 'and you, sir,' he continued, looking at Rohan, 'could I have your tickets and passports? Thanks.'

He checked everything quickly, stamped their tickets, put tags on their luggage, and then said, 'Okay! Now, what kind of seating would you like?'

Rohan looked at the others questioningly, but they shrugged, content to leave the decision to him.

'May we have two window seats one behind the other and the seats next to them?' asked Rohan.

'Sure thing,' said the officer. 'Your idea about seating is a good one, because I'll mark the third seat in each row as "preferably not to be used" – the flight isn't very full tonight. Right! I've given you seats A and B in row nine, as well as row ten A and B. Would you like the same kind of seating on the Qantas flight?'

'Yes, please,' said Rohan.

The officer booked their seats, handed Rohan their boarding passes, tickets and passports and said, 'You'll be boarding at gate number 20 and should go to the lounge by 12:45 at the latest – it's now 11:45 – and you'll need your boarding passes and passports for immigration. Once you enter the lounge, you'll need just your boarding passes.'

They thanked the officer and he wished them a lovely holiday.

Once past immigration, they went through the gates marked for passengers only.

'Now for grub,' said Nimal, 'but perhaps we should first find gate number 20, and see if there's a restaurant close to it.'

The airport was very user-friendly, and there were signs to just about everything.

'There – gates 15 to 20 on the left,' said Rohan, pointing. 'There's a sign for the restaurants, too. Let's go!'

They found a nice restaurant, had a good meal and then walked towards the gates.

'There's our gate,' cried Gina, excitedly, 'and our plane's already parked. Wow! It's humongous and, gosh, there's no one else there. Does that mean we'll have the plane all to ourselves?'

'No, of course not, Gina,' said Rohan with a laugh. 'See, there's no one in the lounge yet – we've got ten minutes to go. People like to visit the duty free shops before the flight.'

'Yeah,' said Nimal, 'wait and see, Gina. A jumbo can carry 400 people or so and, though the officer said the flight was not full, I'm sure there'll be plenty of people on the plane.'

At 12:45, three airline officers came up and started checking in the passengers. The lounge filled up gradually and then a voice announced over the loudspeaker that passengers could now prepare to board the plane.

The children picked up their bags and waited excitedly for their turn. With Rohan in the lead and Nimal bringing up the rear, the Patels reached the door to the plane.

'Good evening, sir,' said a smiling flight attendant to Rohan. 'May I see your boarding pass, please?'

'Hi – we're all together,' said Rohan, indicating the others and showing her their passes.

She smiled at them and said, 'Just turn right here and someone will assist you.'

Following her directions, they soon found their seats.

'Are you folks okay?' asked a flight attendant, coming up when he noticed them.

'Yes, thanks,' said Rohan.

The flight attendant, who was over six feet tall, helped the boys to put away their hand luggage.

The children sat down. They were on the left side of the plane when facing the cockpit, and Gina had the window seat, with Nimal beside her, while Anu and Rohan sat right behind them, with Anu in the window seat.

'This is great,' said Rohan, stretching luxuriously. 'I've got lots of room for my legs compared to the smaller planes we've travelled in.'

'Wow, isn't this neat?' said Gina, bouncing excitedly in her seat.

'Yeah – do you need help with your seat belt, Gina?' asked Nimal fastening his own.

'Just a bit, please. I've put it on, but it's loose.'

Nimal leaned over and showed her how to tighten the belt. So far no one had taken the seats next to Nimal or Rohan.

'When will the plane start moving?' asked Gina.

'Soon,' said Nimal. 'Look, the "fasten your seat belts" sign is on.'

An announcement was made a few minutes later, 'Crew, please secure the doors.'

Flight attendants moved down the aisles, ensuring that seats were in the upright position, seat belts fastened, and luggage bins closed safely.

A cheery voice announced that he was the captain and welcomed them on board. He explained that they would be flying at an altitude of 36,000 feet and would reach Singapore in approximately four hours and fifteen minutes of flying time.

'Gosh, look,' said Gina, 'the plane's been moving all the time he was talking.'

'Yeah – taxiing to the runway,' said Nimal, looking out of the window. 'Just look at the size of those wings, yaar – they're humongous!' he said to Rohan.

'They sure are,' said Rohan, equally awed by the size of the plane. 'I must learn more about aerodynamics.'

'Me, too,' said Nimal.

'Crew, please take your seats in preparation for take-off,' came the captain's voice.

The children tensed in anticipation. They were actually going to take off in a few minutes on their first leg to 'the land down under'.

The plane taxied to the runway for take-off, came to a complete standstill and revved up its powerful engines. It began its run, gathering speed, and then they were in the air and could see the ground falling away rapidly as they rose higher and higher.

'Awesome!' said Rohan. 'I wish I could be a pilot as well as a detective!'

'You should be a flying detective and then you can take us all over the world! We could solve mysteries as we travel,' said Anu with a chuckle.

The seat belt signs went off and flight attendants began serving the passengers with juice and asking them what kind of meal they would like. It was 3 a.m.

The children had something to eat and drink, though Gina was getting sleepy and did not eat a lot.

'Gina,' said Nimal, 'no one's in this third seat so you can stretch out and go to sleep – we'll strap you in. I'll sit in the window seat.'

The little girl agreed and was soon fast asleep, snuggled warmly under a blanket. The others were tired, too, and fell asleep shortly afterwards. Anu only woke up when a flight attendant shook her gently by the shoulder.

'Sorry to wake you, dear,' she said, 'but I think you and the others should get up now and have something to drink. We'll be landing in Singapore in an hour.'

'Gosh, thanks a ton,' said Anu, rubbing her eyes sleepily. 'I'll wake the others.'

She nudged Rohan, who woke up quickly, and then woke up Gina and Nimal.

A drink of hot chocolate and some biscuits revived them, and by the time they were finished, the pilot was announcing that they would be landing at Singapore International Airport in five minutes and thanked everyone for flying with them.

The touchdown was very smooth, and soon the youngsters were making their way out of the plane and to the check-in counter for Qantas. Once that was done, they bought a telephone card and went to the pay phones.

They called all their parents and then Rohan and Anu hurried to the duty free shops while Nimal put Gina, who was once again fast asleep, onto the trolley with their hand luggage and made his way to the boarding lounge.

Rohan and Anu quickly picked up a couple of nice T-shirts for Jack and Mike, as well as a few souvenir items for others they might meet, and then joined Nimal. The boys were fine, but Anu was quite bushed.

'Don't wake Gina,' said Rohan, as the announcement to board the plane came over the loudspeakers. 'I'll carry her if you manage the bags, Nimal; Anu, here are the boarding passes.'

'No problemo,' they agreed.

Once on the plane, they were lucky to have two rows of seats to themselves again. Though their flight was taking off at 10:45 a.m., with the time difference and lack of sleep, only Rohan managed to stay awake until the plane took off, and then he also fell asleep.

By two in the afternoon, however, all of them were wide awake, and extremely hungry.

'I'm starving,' groaned Gina. 'Have we missed dinner?'

'It's lunchtime, honey,' said the friendly flight attendant, who had come up when she saw that the children were awake. 'Are you the Patel family?'

'Yes, we are,' said Anu. 'How did you know?'

'We were warned that there were four enormous appetites on this flight, and I figured they must belong to you kids – right?' she said with a smile.

'You bet!' said Nimal. 'Can we really get lots to eat? I'm starving!'

'I'll be right back,' said the flight attendant, bustling away.

The youngsters had a delicious meal.

'Would you like some more?' asked the flight attendant when she saw they had finished. 'There's plenty more chocolate cake for anyone who fancies it.'

'Yes, please,' said Gina at once. She was a chocolate cake fanatic. 'I would love another piece – if you're sure it's okay.'

'Of course, dear,' said the flight attendant, 'and how about you others?'

'Er . . . I wouldn't mind another piece – just to keep Gina company, of course,' said Nimal.

They got their chocolate cake and then pulled out books as there was nothing to see outside the window, other than clouds. The plane was not very full, and was carrying only 300 passengers, so there were lots of empty seats.

'Ah – here are a couple of seats,' said a male voice just behind Rohan.

Rohan glanced over his shoulder briefly as someone bumped heavily into his seat, and saw two men sit down right behind him and Anu. One was about five foot eleven inches tall, and very broad, while the other, though taller, was extremely skinny. They took no notice of the children, and did not even apologize for bumping Rohan's seat.

'So, Darrel,' said the first man, lowering his voice, 'what luck did you have when you talked to Jack about the Conservation?'

Rohan pricked up his ears. He could hear them quite clearly, and though he did not mean to eavesdrop, he wondered if they knew Jack. They sounded Australian.

'None at all, John,' said Darrel. 'In fact, he was very stubborn and unwilling to co-operate or see our point of view. He said it was cruel to have a park for animals just so that people could come and shoot them. He also said that if we were thinking of starting up another organization for people to hunt dolphins and whales, he would fight us to the bitter end.'

A flight attendant came round with drinks and the men stopped talking for a few minutes. Rohan nudged Anu, who was engrossed in a book, and whispered to her in Hindi, saying, 'Listen to the conversation behind us.' Anu raised her eyebrows, but listened as the men continued their conversation.

'But wasn't he interested in the money you offered him? He could use it for a conservation somewhere else instead of bothering with all his fundraising nonsense,' said John.

'He isn't concerned about the money at all. When I mentioned it he accused us of trying to bribe him. He also said that the purpose of fundraising was not only to raise money, but to create awareness of the cause,' said Darrel bitterly.

'That man will ruin us,' growled John. 'We'll have to find other ways of dealing with him. Once we get back we'll put our heads together and see what we come up with. I'm not going to let him chase us away from the area! Ever since he and his stupid group came to the Gold Coast with their brainwave of starting a conservation for sea creatures, we've had fewer people visiting the lodge.' He paused and continued, 'Here's an idea – why don't we rope in Alastair and Eugene to do some brainstorming? They're used to dealing with "problem" folk.'

'There's something in that,' assented Darrel cautiously, 'but let's be careful this time, John. We don't want the cops on our case for assault and battery again – we just managed to get them off our backs the last time those two had a brainwave!'

'Yeah, yeah, okay,' grunted John. 'Don't be so cowardly, Darrel.'

The men discussed a few more matters, mainly about staffing, and then moved away, presumably returning to their own seats.

'Don't say anything just now,' whispered Rohan in Hindi. 'I'll check where they're seated first.' He got up and said, in a normal tone of voice, 'I'm just going to the bathroom.'

He moved towards the bathroom at the rear and spotted the men easily enough – they were seated about ten rows behind the kids, across the aisle from each other. Rohan took a quick mental picture of what they looked like, finished with the bathroom and returned to his seat.

'Okay, we can talk safely,' said Rohan to Anu. He tapped Nimal on the shoulder and said, 'We've got news.'

Gina and Nimal leant over the seats and Rohan and Anu repeated softly, in Hindi, what they had heard.

'They're obviously talking about Uncle Jack's new Conservation,' said Rohan. 'Though I don't want to jump to conclusions just because I heard Uncle Jack's name, everything adds up – the Gold Coast, conservation, sea creatures – and I'm sure there can't be two people named Jack starting up new conservations in the same area.'

'Horrible men, to actually have a hunting lodge,' muttered Anu angrily. 'I thought those places were dying out with all the awareness and the push towards conservation.'

'Yeah, but unfortunately there are still places all over the world where people can hunt animals,' said Nimal in a low voice. 'Look at our own country.'

'I don't think we should discuss this any more at the moment,' said Rohan. 'There are too many people around and we don't know who else understands Hindi. We'll wait till we get a chance to talk to Uncle Jack.'

The others agreed. They were all upset, and though they tried to distract themselves from thinking about it too much, it was hard to focus on something else.

Fortunately, a comic movie was scheduled to start soon and Rohan suggested that they put on their headsets and watch it.

After the enjoyable movie and dinner, the youngsters fell asleep for a couple of hours until Rohan woke them.

'We'll be landing in Brisbane soon,' he said. 'Let's make sure we've got everything.'

They organized themselves and then settled down to look out for the airport.

'There, you can see lots of lights,' said Gina, peering excitedly out of her window. 'Is that the airport, Nimal?'

'Probably,' said Nimal, leaning over to look out of the window. 'Okay, folks, seats upright, et cetera.'

The announcement came over the air a few minutes later, and soon they had landed smoothly and taxied to a halt. The doors were opened and the children disembarked.

CHAPTER 4

Old Friends and New

They made their way to the carousel and waited for their baggage to arrive. The boys got a couple of trolleys and Gina perched on one.

'Oh, look!' said Gina suddenly, pointing behind the others.

They turned, and then burst out laughing.

'Isn't he adorable!' said Anu. 'I love his little outfit – it says "the fruit and veggie dog". I wonder what he's doing?'

They got their answer a few minutes later. The dog, on a leash held by a man in uniform, was going up to each individual's hand luggage, sniffing at it and then moving on. They watched curiously.

'He's stopped at that person's baggage,' said Nimal, 'and is sitting down.'

The officer spoke to the man, who opened his hand baggage. The officer checked it, pulled out a couple of apples, and pointed to a bin. The man went off to throw the apples away and the fruit and veggie dog moved on, sniffing at more bags.

'Oh,' said Anu. 'Remember those cards we had to fill out before we landed? They warned us not to carry any fruit or other edibles off the plane and I bet this little dog is checking for food in everyone's hand luggage.'

As they continued to watch, the dog came up to them, sniffed at their bags, and then, yielding to Nimal's charisma, gave him a lick, waving his tail madly.

The officer was astonished. 'He's never done that before,' he said to the children. 'I can't believe it – these dogs are very well trained.'

'Nimal has an extraordinary way with all animals,' said Rohan. 'They simply can't resist him.'

'I can see that,' said the officer. 'Lucky boy! I have to carry on now – have a good holiday.'

They waved goodbye to him and the little dog, and watched the animal sniff out more veggies and fruit from other hand luggage. Their baggage had still not been unloaded from the plane.

'Hey – another dog,' said Nimal, spotting a big black one this time, held on a leash by another officer. 'Wonder what this chap's trained for?'

This dog was also sniffing at bags and, naturally, he, too, stopped to lick Nimal, before moving on to two teenagers standing close to the children. The dog sniffed at their bags, gave a small bark and sat down, looking up at his master.

'Could you please open your bag?' requested the officer.

'W-we don't have anything b-but clothes and s-stuff,' said the boy quickly.

'I'd still like to check, please,' said the officer.

Nervously the boy opened the bag, while the girl watched anxiously. The officer pulled out a packet that was wrapped in plastic, sniffed at it, and then turned to the teenagers.

'I'll have to ask you to come with me please,' he said. 'Walk this way.'

He led them off towards a room. The teens looked scared.

'Why did he take them away?' asked Gina.

'I think that was a drug-sniffing dog,' said Rohan, 'and I guess those two were smuggling dope into the country.'

'They didn't look much older than us,' said Anu, 'eighteen or nineteen at the most. I wonder if there's a drug problem here.'

'Possibly,' said Rohan. 'I'm sure lots of people here, too, think that drugs will help them to forget their worries.'

'Yeah – luckily our parents and schools keep warning us about drugs being dangerous,' said Nimal.

'Also, that you can't run away from your problems because they'll always come with you,' quoted Gina, who was just learning about drugs and other similar issues.

'Right, Gina,' said Anu. 'I see you've been reading the book Mum gave you earlier this year.'

'We're also learning about drug abuse in my class,' said Gina.

'Oh, look – here come the bags!' said Nimal.

'Who's coming to meet us?' asked Anu. 'Uncle Jack and Mike?'

'Yeah, I think so,' said Rohan. 'I hope our bags are in the first batch so that we can get out soon. It's already 11:30 p.m., Brisbane time, and I think we're all ready for bed.' He glanced at Gina who, though wide awake and eagerly looking out for their suitcases, was yawning and looking rather pale.

'Mmmm – I'm also pretty bushed,' said Anu.

'Our bags are coming,' said Gina excitedly. 'I can see the blue ribbons Anu tied on them. But there are only three – do you think they lost one?'

'I'm sure the fourth one will come along,' said Nimal, moving to the carousel with Rohan so that they could lift the bags off.

The boys pulled off the suitcases, piled them on trolleys, and just then Anu spotted the last bag. Rohan put it on the trolley, and they went through immigration and then walked towards the exit.

'Look out for Mike,' said Rohan. 'We should be able to spot him easily – he's so tall.'

'There, there!' squealed Gina, jumping down from the trolley, 'I can see them both.'

Sure enough, Jack and Mike, waving madly, were right in front of the crowd waiting outside the gates to welcome family and friends.

'Uncle Jack! Mike!' shrieked Gina, running towards them and leaping up into Jack's arms. The others were right behind her.

'Hello, honey!' said Jack giving her a big hug and a scratchy kiss through his beard.

'Oh, Mike, it's fantastic to see you,' said Gina, turning to hug him, too. Mike swung her high above his head, grinning with pleasure. He was thrilled to see all of them again, and had missed them a great deal.

There were hugs all around, Gina was perched on Mike's shoulders and they were all talking, nineteen to the dozen.

'I have a surprise for you in the car,' said Jack, as they took a lift to the parking lot below. 'Can you guess what it is?'

'A dolphin in the back seat!' said Nimal with a grin.

'A baby seal,' squeaked Gina, 'a teeny, weeny one.'

'Give us a hint, Uncle Jack,' said Rohan.

'Well – it's two people whom you've heard of but haven't met,' said Jack.

'I know,' said Anu, her eyes gleaming, 'your nieces from Canada! Right?'

'Right on, mate! What a good guess!' said Jack. 'Yes, Amy and Michelle are waiting in the Land Rover for you. They wanted to give us time on our own before they joined us.'

'When did they arrive?' asked Rohan. 'The APs didn't say a word about them.'

'Last night,' said Jack, 'and I asked your parents not to say anything as I wanted to surprise you.'

'It's a wonderful surprise,' said Rohan, grinning broadly. 'We've heard so much about them and now we're actually going to meet them.'

'They've heard lots about you, too,' said Mike smiling. 'Oh, don't worry – I've only told them the good things – so far!'

The children were thrilled. They had heard a lot about Amy and Michelle and seen photographs of them, and now they would actually be spending a holiday together. What fun!

As the lift stopped and they got out, the children looked around eagerly. Two girls were walking towards them.

Mike put Gina down.

'Here they are,' said Jack. 'I know you won't need introductions. Oh, by the way, Michelle is usually called Mich.'

'Hi! I'm Amy, and you must be Anu, right?' said Amy, greeting Anu with a hug and a kiss. She turned to the others greeting each of them by name and giving them a hug and a kiss, too. Mich followed suit.

'I feel as if I've known you for years,' said Anu with a grin, feeling instinctively that they would get along well.

'Yeah,' said Nimal, looking admiringly at Amy's beautiful dark brown hair which reached down to her waist, 'and I'm sure you'll lend me your hair when it gets c-c-c-cold.'

'Sure thing,' said Amy with a grin. 'Uncle Jack's already warned me about you, Nimal. He said you were the biggest tease I would ever come across. He said . . .' she trailed off with a laugh.

Nimal, pretending to hide behind Mike, muttered, 'And I thought Uncle Jack was a good guy and would only say *nice* things about me. I'm shattered, Uncle Jack.'

'No worries – you'll get over it, mate,' said Jack with a laugh. 'Now, into the vehicle – pronto! Time to get you home – it's way past your bedtime.'

Gina and Mich eyed each other. Mich, also nine years old and a bit taller than Gina, had short, curly ash-blonde hair and bright blue eyes which were currently rather sleepy. She was a little shy, but eager to make friends with this girl about whom she had heard so many good things. Gina liked Mich, too, but was quite exhausted by now and did not say a lot.

They reached the vehicle, Mike and the boys loaded the luggage into it and everyone clambered in, Mike and Nimal sitting up front with Jack.

'Where do you live, Uncle Jack?' asked Rohan, as they set off. 'Dad said you were fairly close to the new Conservation.'

'That's right, Rohan,' said Jack. 'We live in the Gold Coast area, and will be home soon. The Conservation is a twenty-minute drive away from my place.'

The adults asked for news of friends at the Patiyak Wildlife Conservation Centre in India, and thirty minutes flew by.

'We're nearly home,' said Mike, as the Land Rover turned off the main highway and followed a two-lane road for a short distance.

'Here we are,' said Jack, turning into a driveway. 'You'll be asleep in no time at all.'

He pulled up in front of a large house, which looked friendly and comfortable.

'Just take your hand luggage and don't worry about the rest,' said Mike. 'We'll take care of it.'

Everyone jumped out of the vehicle and the youngsters were ushered into the house.

'Hello, children – welcome to Brisbane,' said a soft Australian voice.

The Patels turned to see a petite older lady, with snow-white hair, smiling at them.

'This is my Aunty Meg,' said Jack. 'She looks after the home and keeps me in order; I don't know how we'd manage without her. She's also a Larkin.'

Jack introduced the children and then continued, 'Now, if it's okay with all of you, let's say goodnight and get you off to bed. I'll call your parents, and we'll see you in the morning – whatever time you wake up. No rush. It's great to have you here at last.'

They thanked him and followed Ms. Larkin upstairs, where they were soon ensconced in two beautiful bedrooms, beside each other, with a connecting door. Glasses of hot chocolate were gratefully received by the children.

The Larkin girls drank their chocolate with the Patels, then said goodnight and went into a room across the hall.

'There are two bathrooms just down the hallway,' said Ms. Larkin, as she bustled about the room to make sure they had everything they needed.

'Thank you so much, Ms. Larkin . . .' began Rohan.

'Do call me Aunty Meg, if you please,' interrupted Ms. Larkin. 'I feel as if I know you – Jack and Mike are always talking about you.'

'Sure thing, Aunty Meg!' said Nimal with a grin, and the others all said 'Goodnight and thank you, Aunty Meg'.

'Sleep well, and please make yourselves at home,' said Aunty Meg.

She went out and, after a quick wash and change, they tumbled into bed and fell asleep immediately. The trip had completely exhausted them!

****

'Ouch,' yelped Nimal the next morning as he rolled off his bed with a bump. 'Where am I?'

His yell woke Rohan, who sat up and looked at him with a grin. 'Man! Nearly fourteen years old and *still* can't get out of bed properly. We're at Uncle Jack's, yaar. Good grief – it's 11 o'clock!'

They got out of bed and went over to the window.

'Wow, we're right on the banks of a river,' said Rohan. 'Let's explore.'

'Wake the girls first,' said Nimal.

'Right,' agreed Rohan, knocking on the connecting door.

'Come in,' said Anu. Both girls were already up and dressed.

'Good morning, boys. We peeped in but you were sound asleep so we didn't disturb you,' said Anu.

'Yeah, and did you see the river?' asked Gina, who was full of energy once more, though still pale.

'We sure did,' said Nimal. 'Right, we'll be ready in a jiffy, and then we'll look for the dining room – I'm starving!'

They rejoined the girls quickly and went in search of the others. As they hesitated at the top of the staircase, Jack's cheerful voice hailed them from below.

'G'day, mates! I hope you had a good rest and are ready for a big brunch. Come on down. Everyone's waiting to meet you.'

They ran downstairs and he led them into a large dining room where Mike, Aunty Meg and the Larkin girls were already seated. There were also four other people they did not know.

'These four are part of our Management Team,' said Jack, 'and as they already know about you, I'll introduce them – oh, and they prefer to be called by their first names. So, let's see – starting with that short, skinny chap over there – he's Okanu.'

'Hi, folks,' said Okanu, grinning from ear to ear as he came over to shake hands with them.

'But . . . but . . .' stammered Gina, as she craned her neck to look up at the African who was nearly seven feet tall, very broad and fit. 'He's not short at all, Uncle Jack. He's nearly twice my height!'

'You know what Jack's like, Gina,' said Okanu, bending almost double to shake hands with the little girl. 'And he's jealous because he and I can only talk at the same level when I'm seated and he's standing!'

'Yes, that's the only way I'm *willing* to talk to him,' said Jack with a grin. 'Otherwise, he gives me a pain in the neck. As our engineer, Okanu is responsible for all the technical and mechanical jobs that need to be carried out. Of course, as everyone knows, I would be better at those jobs myself, but I like to make others feel wanted.'

Okanu grinned and the others roared with laughter. They obviously knew Jack well and, while they had a great deal of respect and affection for him, they were also familiar with his technical and mechanical skills – or rather, *lack* of them!

'The ugly-looking one is Padmini,' said Jack, pointing to a beautiful young woman. 'You just watch out for her! She's dangerous! The guys don't fall for her looks, they fall for her karate chops! She's a karate expert – has her second level brown belt.'

'Hello, folks,' said Padmini in a soft voice. 'I'm responsible for the money in this venture. And, Jack, if you don't watch it, you won't get paid this month!'

Jack grimaced at her. 'She's our accountant.' He continued, 'That chap over there is Czainski. He graduated from Oxford with *only* two PhDs – in conservation and natural sciences! Since we don't like to hurt his feelings about his lack of academic qualifications, we give him the task of being our chief fundraiser. He makes speeches, organizes events, and generally rolls in the money.'

'Hello, folks,' said Czainski, speaking with a marked British accent. 'I am awfully pleased to meet you, and have heard a great deal about you from Jack. I am having a tough time with him – that strange dialect he calls English is quite appalling.'

'Whadya mean, mate?' said Jack. 'Me English is as good as yers.'

'The first time he asked me for "a bisin to wash me fice in, maite", I thought he was talking about a bison, and I told him that the animal would probably butt him if he tried to wash his face in it. That was before I realized that he meant *basin*, and since then I have been striving to teach him English, without much success, needless to say!'

Everyone laughed and Mike teased, 'Hey, Czainski, what about being politically correct and not making fun of people's accents? After all, you're always reminding us about this in our communications.'

'Well, if Jack would stop abusing us,' said Czainski, 'which is *also* politically incorrect, my lad, perhaps I would be PC where he's concerned. On the other hand, if we can't laugh at ourselves and our friends, life would be dull, indeed – wouldn't it?'

'Pax! Pax!' laughed Mike. 'I have to agree with you, just for once! Patels, you'll soon discover that most Australians have a good sense of humour and love to tease each other – the way we do.'

Jack introduced the last person in the room.

'Now, being PC in our spelling, that tiny *womyn* is Jalila. She's responsible for all the shows which we plan to hold at the Conservation and is a qualified actress. She is fluent in English, French and Arabic. Her husband, Czainski, loves her best when she's asleep – because then she finally stops talking.'

'Hello, there,' said Jalila, smiling and speaking very rapidly. 'I guess you know what your Uncle Jack's like and won't believe most of what he says, right? Welcome to Brisbane and the Gold Coast. I'm looking forward to getting to know all of you. I'm especially keen on talking to you, Anu, because I hear you write stories. I wonder if you've ever thought of writing a play for seals and . . .'

She trailed off as the room erupted in laughter at her rapid-fire chatter. 'Oh, well, let's talk later, Anu, when these morons are not around,' she finished with a grin, throwing a napkin ring at Jack, 'and I don't *care* if I'm not PC!'

'Let's have brunch,' said Aunty Meg. 'Come on children, serve yourselves.'

A large side table was laid out in buffet style, with hot plates under the dishes to keep the food warm. Soon everyone was seated around the table eating hungrily.

'I couldn't do without my Management Team,' said Jack. 'As you know, Mike's our general manager, and you'll meet Helen on Monday – she's the office manager. And, of course, there's my assistant, Monique, and lots of other staff on the Conservation, plus all the volunteers and fundraisers.'

'Can we go to the Conservation today, Uncle Jack?' asked Nimal. 'And, also, when do we get Hunter?'

'Let's deal with Hunter first,' said Jack. 'Monique called the vet yesterday, and he said Hunter was fine. His quarantine is over on Sunday night and we'll collect him then.'

'Oh, goody,' said Gina. 'We really miss him – he's our dog,' she explained to Mich, 'and we love him a lot.'

'Today,' continued Jack, 'since all of you, including Amy and Mich, have had long journeys, we think you should relax around the house, have a good nap in the afternoon, and an early night. The time difference and jet lag are sure to catch up with you otherwise.'

'And you can spend time getting to know each other, too,' said Aunty Meg.

'Sounds great,' said Rohan, 'so can we come to the Conservation tomorrow?'

'I didn't want you kids to start *work* too soon,' said Jack, with a grin, 'and I wanted you to see some of the delights Brisbane offers, not just our Conservation. So, I've planned a couple of tours for you on Saturday and Sunday.'

'Wow – thanks, Uncle Jack,' said Anu. 'Where are we going?'

'Well, tomorrow you'll visit the Sunshine Coast, which is an hour's drive north of Brisbane; then on Sunday you do a tour of Brisbane City, go for a ride on the City Cat, and Mike and I will pick you up afterwards and take you out to dinner.'

'How do we go on these tours, Uncle?' asked Amy.

'We have superb organized tours starting from the Roma Street bus station which is situated in the heart of Brisbane. Mike will take you there tomorrow morning and the tour guides will look after you from that point on. Since all of you are pretty used to looking after yourselves and one another, I'm sure you won't have any problems. You'll have our phone numbers, Aunty Meg has a spare mobile phone which she'll give you and, in an emergency, you can contact any of us.'

'What's there to see in the Sunshine Coast?' asked Nimal. 'Is it also a surfer's paradise like the Gold Coast?'

'Not really,' said Okanu, 'and actually the tour takes you to a couple of other places on the way to the Sunshine Coast. The coast itself has a large "Underwater World" as they call it – a massive tank – you go underground into a kind of glass tunnel with the fish swimming above and on either side of you.' ·

'Gee, does that mean there'll be dolphins swimming above us, Uncle Jack?' asked Mich, who had not spoken so far.

'No, love,' said Jack. 'No dolphins. But there'll be stingrays, some types of sharks, and hundreds of other varieties of fish.'

'What are the other places?' asked Rohan.

'You'll be visiting the Big Pineapple, the Busy Bee Farm and Glenforest Sanctuary, and we're not going to give you details about those places, because I want you to have some surprises,' concluded Jack with a grin.

They laughed. It would be fun to see some of the other attractions in Brisbane.

'I guess everyone's finished eating for now,' said Aunty Meg, a while later. 'A last piece of chocolate cake, anyone? It will go to waste otherwise.'

'Yes, please, Aunty Meg,' said Nimal, very politely. 'And, speaking for Gina and Mich, too, we would hate you to feel that no one loves your chocolate cake. It's simply delish!'

'Get along with you,' laughed Aunty Meg, dividing it into three and handing it out.

'Now, kids – when you've spoken to your respective parents, let's go out into the garden and catch up on news,' suggested Jack when everyone had finished eating.

'Great idea, Jack,' said Okanu. 'Mike, Czainski, let's put some chairs out.' They went off.

Aunty Meg supervised the helpers – two men and two women who lived on the premises. She also dealt with the numerous calls that came in for Jack and the others, who all lived in the house at present. It was a large house with a multitude of bedrooms. There was plenty of room for everyone and also room for any visitors who turned up, as they frequently did. Jack was a generous host.

Jack took the Patels to the study and both sets of parents were called, after which they joined the others on the lawn.

'It's great to have a river at your doorstep, Uncle Jack,' said Anu. 'What's it called?'

'The Moosanagi,' said Jack, 'and it's our main river. When we return from work this evening, I'll take you for a boat ride.'

'Cool!' said Amy. 'Can we swim in it?'

'Not really,' said Okanu. 'It has strong currents and is extremely deep. Also, if you don't have a powerful motor on your boat, the current will drag a boat along quite rapidly!'

The children wandered around, exploring the grounds, checking out the boat and looking at the neighbouring houses.

'Good grief!' said Rohan suddenly to Nimal, as they were examining the boat. 'I nearly forgot about those chaps! Come on, yaar – we've got to tell Uncle Jack about the conversation on the plane last night.'

Calling to the others, they ran back to where the adults were seated. The others followed, wondering what had happened.

When they were all seated on the grass, Rohan began.

'Uncle Jack,' he said, 'yesterday on the plane we heard a strange discussion between two chaps, and you need to know about it.'

He and Anu told the adults what they had heard.

'More trouble,' said Jack. 'Those men were probably John Ingram and Darrel Owen, and they own "Wilderness Adventures", also located in the Gold Coast.'

The Gold Coast was a great tourist attraction because of Surfer's Paradise, and millions of people came there every year to surf and enjoy the many attractions the coast held. John's business had flourished for the past five years, but ever since Jack Larkin and others had raised awareness of the cruelty to animals and the desperate need for conservation, John's lodge had suffered a setback.

'What did they look like, Rohan?' asked Jack.

'Hmmm . . .' said Rohan, squinting into space for a moment, 'One was about five foot eleven inches, very broad but not fit, he had a big belly, tanned skin, blond hair and blue eyes.'

'John Ingram, for sure,' said Czainski.

'The second chap was taller than him, perhaps about six foot three inches or so, and he was very skinny and pale. He had brown hair and eyes.'

'Darrel Owen – John's best friend and manager of the lodge,' said Jack. 'I thought so! Well, as they say, forewarned is forearmed, and we'll certainly look out for them. We'll warn Helen and the others at our staff meeting this afternoon,' he continued. 'However, it's now 1 p.m. and time we went back to work and you young folk had a good nap.'

'What time will all of you return this evening?' inquired Aunty Meg.

'I'll be back around 6:30,' said Jack, 'so that I can take my nieces and nephews for a boat ride.'

'The rest of us will probably only return in time for dinner, Aunty Meg,' said Mike. 'We've got a lot of stuff to do at the site. Jack, a word with you before we leave.'

They walked off together, while the others followed in groups. The children said goodbye to the adults, and then dispersed to their rooms for a nap, which they were surprised to find they badly needed!

CHAPTER 5

Getting to Know Each Other

Anu woke up with a start – she had been dreaming of John Ingram who was chasing the dolphins with a gun, while the dolphins were waterskiing beautifully! She looked at her watch and was puzzled for a moment before she realized that she had not reset it to Australian time. She adjusted it to 3:30 p.m. Gina had not moved.

'I'll let her sleep – she's exhausted,' thought Anu. 'I'll see if any of the others are awake.'

Peeping into the boys' room, she grinned at Rohan who had been gazing out of the window, but turned as the door opened. 'Nimal still dead to the world?' she whispered, and Rohan nodded. They left the room quietly.

Amy came out of her room just then. 'Let's go to the library,' she suggested. 'The others can join us when they're up.'

'Good idea,' said Rohan.

They went downstairs and found themselves in a large room with bookshelves lining three of the walls, and an eclectic selection of books. Anu was in heaven! She left the other two, and wandered around the room, checking out the books and tuning into their conversation every now and then.

Rohan and Amy seated themselves in a couple of comfortable armchairs.

'You're much older than I thought, Rohan,' said Amy, who found Rohan's looks and personality very appealing.

'I'm fifteen,' said Rohan, 'but everyone thinks I'm older because I'm tall. Aren't we almost the same age?'

'Oh, I guess so,' said Amy in surprise. 'I turned fifteen last month on the twenty-sixth. When were you fifteen? I figured you must be at least seventeen or so.'

'I'm a week older than you, then,' said Rohan with a grin. 'My birthday's on the eighteenth of November – so you'd better treat me with respect since I'm not only older than you, but much bigger!'

Amy laughed. She was just five foot three. 'Why, will you give me a karate kick if I don't behave?' she teased, smiling at him mischievously.

'No – because we've been brought up never to hit girls, or rather, *womyn* to be PC,' said Rohan, 'but I would definitely set Nimal on you. He's a wicked tease and would play some horrible trick. Do you know what he did to a chap at our school last spring? This chap . . .'

Rohan told her the story of Nimal's trick and had Amy in fits of laughter.

Anu joined them as Amy brought up the subject of what they each wanted to do after high school.

'I want to be a psychologist and work on therapeutic healing by bringing dolphins and humans together,' said Amy. 'What about you, Anu? Rohan?'

'Wow! Fascinating! I'm going to be an author – I'll write books about all of you,' said Anu. 'I've always dreamed of writing books, and hope I can afford to follow my dream. I know it doesn't pay well until you're a well-known author, but I'm willing to do other work, to keep body and soul together, till I succeed with my books.'

'Nimal and I'll look after you till then, sis,' said Rohan with a grin. 'You'll be so busy dreaming of your books that your body will be wandering around looking for its lost soul! A real "soul-searching experience" that'll be. Actually,' he continued, turning to Amy, 'though she talks like a book, at times she's extremely logical and clear thinking, but far too intellectual for her own good. And she can cook, when the need arises – occasionally, very occasionally! But emotionally – though she's good at tuning in to others' emotions, her own lag far behind her intellect, so she's trying to get in touch with them, and keeps sending them emails!'

Anu chuckled as she threw a cushion at Rohan. 'Huh, you're the one to talk about *me* being intellectual?' she said. 'Amy, this chap is so academic at times that we're just grateful he wants to be a detective like our friend Peter, instead of studying and living in the world of academia. He's not *all* bad, though,' she continued, grinning affectionately at her brother. 'We're training him well and he's improving – though his progress is painfully slow!'

Amy burst out laughing and Rohan threw the cushion back at his sister.

'Do you two always go on at each other like this?' asked Amy enviously. 'I wish I had brothers, too – you all seem to be really close, even with your cousin, Nimal.'

'We are very close,' said Rohan. 'Nimal's our *brother* as far as we're concerned – and he feels the same way.'

'Well, you and Nimal certainly look very alike – feature-wise,' said Amy. 'Come to think of it, other than for height, hair and personalities, you could pass for twins!'

'True,' said Anu. 'Let me bore you with a brief description of each of us. I've already told you about Rohan. Nimal is intellectual and has a brilliant brain, but he's not very academic. He wants to be a conservationist, like Dad and Uncle Jack. He has the most extraordinary charisma where animals are concerned, which you'll see in action soon enough. Rohan's told you about me. Gina, we feel, is going to be a musical genius. She's quite precocious for her age – probably because she has to hang around with us older ones, but despite the fact that, after our trip here, she is now determined to become a pilot of a jumbo jet, she adores her music. She's not at all academic, but good at sports and writing poetry, which, so far, has been mostly nonsense verse. We're all independent – extremely so – and love books, animals, travel, adventure and meeting people from other countries. Now, your turn!'

'Right! As I said, I want to study psychology,' said Amy. 'I'm not particularly academic but get fair grades in school. I love skiing, both on water and in snow, and I enjoy swimming. I'm very interested in conservation and discrimination issues, and I'm totally crazy about dolphins. Mich is a little shy till she gets to know people. She's brill at all sports, is a fantastic skater and is like a fish in the water, but, like Gina, she's not an academic. She wants to work for Disney and draw cartoons for their animation movies – her drawing is simply out of this world! She and I are also very close, and though we go to different schools at the moment, we'll be at the same one next year. We're both extremely independent, and love books. I know she likes all of you, and she and Gina are already good friends – they were chattering away this morning.'

'Here come the others,' said Rohan, looking around as the door opened and the other three came in. 'Did you have a good nap?'

'Slept like the dead,' said Nimal, still yawning and tripping over the edge of the carpet as he entered. 'Wow, what a fantastic room.' He and Gina wandered around looking at all the books, especially those on the conservation of sea creatures.

'Mich, come over here,' called Gina, looking at a book on dolphins. Mich joined her. 'Look – people are riding on dolphins. Have you seen lots of dolphins?' asked Gina.

'Yes,' said Mich, 'Dad and Mum took us out in a boat on the Pacific ocean, and the dolphins came up and played with us.'

'Gosh, Mich,' said Nimal enviously, 'do you mean you were able to touch them?'

'Not that time,' said Mich, 'but when we went to Stanley Park, in Vancouver, we saw dolphins and were allowed to stroke them. Only for a minute though as so many people wanted to pet them.' She continued, 'I adore them and would love to play with them.'

'Don't worry, Mich,' said Gina, 'Nimal can make any animal come to him, and I'm sure the dolphins at Uncle Jack's Conservation will make friends with him and then we can all play with them.'

'Cool!' said Mich looking up at Nimal in awe. 'Do all animals make friends with you?'

'Well, for some strange reason, they seem to like me,' said Nimal, grinning at her. 'They probably think I look like them and recognize me as a brother!' He made a funny face.

The girls giggled madly. Mich was already comfortable with Anu, and she and Gina had become fast friends. She liked the 'big boys', as she thought of Rohan and Nimal, and was fast losing her shyness with them, too.

'Anu,' said Amy suddenly, 'I remember Uncle Jack saying something about you writing a book. Have you finished it?'

'Oh,' said Anu, looking embarrassed, 'actually, it's half done, but I didn't have much time at school to complete it – so it's on hold till next term.'

'What's it about?' asked Mich.

'An adventure we had last summer hols,' said Anu.

'Tell her the story, please, Anu,' begged Gina, who enjoyed listening to Anu's tales, real or make-believe.

'Later,' promised Anu.

'What's it called?' asked Mich.

'*Peacock Feathers*,' said Anu.

'I'd love to hear it, too, Anu,' said Amy eagerly.

'Maybe you can tell everyone the story tonight, Anu,' said Nimal. 'She's a fantastic storyteller and an excellent writer. She'll be famous, mark my words. She also makes wonderful chocolate cake and sandwiches, and I'm going to live with her forever and ever.'

'Okay, Nimal,' said Anu, turning red with embarrassment, 'what exactly are you fishing for?'

'Just a story, *please* . . .' begged Nimal, going down on one knee in front of Anu and clasping his hands together dramatically. Anu promptly pulled his hair.

'You Patels!' said Amy, laughing at the clowning duo. 'You're so British in the way you speak and tease each other – you remind me of the characters in Enid Blyton's stories.'

'I guess we are quite British in that way,' said Anu with a grin. 'After all, India was a British colony for years. How do you know the Enid Blyton books? I thought they weren't that popular in Canada and the States.'

'We both love reading adventure stories,' said Amy, 'if they're well written. I guess the English is more formal than ours – but they're great fun!'

'I know we're rather formal, too, at times – but blame the APs for that,' said Anu. 'We grew up reading mainly British authors, though I've also read the *Anne of Green Gables* and *Little House on the Prairie* series – and love them.'

'APs?' asked Mich.

'Aged Parents,' said Rohan, and the Larkins burst out laughing.

'I like that,' chuckled Amy. 'Oh, by the way, I also heard about a group you started for kids who are keen on environmental issues. What's that about and can we join, too?'

'Of course you can,' said Rohan promptly. 'We started it last year and called it "The Junior Environmentalists and Conservationists" – JEACs for short.' (He pronounced it 'Jee-acks'.) 'We try to recruit one other person in school, each term – if you recruit more, that's even better.'

'But how do you recruit people?' asked Mich, looking scared.

'Well, we wear our badges – which are very colourful – and when people ask us about them, and what JEACs stands for, we tell them. If they seem interested, we explain further and give them some literature prepared by us. Also, for our presentations or reports in school, we try and talk about conservation and environmental issues,' said Anu.

'So, did each of you manage to recruit members last term?' asked Amy.

'Actually, we've recruited more than one each, and the total in our schools is now 21 – excluding ourselves,' said Nimal. 'It's great to know that so many people are interested in saving our planet.'

'Awesome!' said Amy enthusiastically. 'Do we have to pay something to join? Can Mich and I join now? How do we get badges?'

'You don't have to pay anything to join – and of course you must become members. You can start a Canadian branch,' said Anu. 'We have extra badges and all you have to do is read the literature and check out our website – http://www.jeacs.com – so that you know what we're trying to achieve. Anyone can make a donation, no fixed amount, whenever they're able to during the year and all the members vote as to which conservation should receive the money each year. However, making donations is not compulsory in order to join. It's more important to spend time and energy in helping conservations and creating awareness among others.'

'You see, we don't want anyone to feel that they *can't* join because they don't have the money,' explained Rohan. 'There are a lot of very poor people in India who are keen on joining and want to help in any way they can, but they can't afford to pay.'

'Gee – please count us in,' said Amy. 'And since we can easily afford to donate some of our pocket money, I'll pass that on, too.'

'Superfantabulous! I'll get your badges after tea,' said Anu.

'Don't give us the money, though,' said Nimal. 'Start up the group in Canada, and donate the money to a conservation there.'

'Will do,' said Amy, while Mich clapped her hands happily.

'And now,' continued Nimal, looking at Amy, 'I don't want to seem greedy, but I'm a growing boy and all that sort of thing . . . do you know if people in Brisbane believe in having tea? I'm simply . . .'

He stopped with a laugh as the others shouted, '*Starving!*'

'Good!' said a cheerful voice from the doorway. 'I have an enormous tea waiting to be consumed. Come and get it!'

'You're a lifesaver, Aunty Meg!' said Nimal, bouncing up to her and giving her a big hug.

'Get along with you, Nimal,' said Aunty Meg. 'You can't butter me up.'

'I was only planning to butter the bread, Aunty divine,' said Nimal cheekily, as they followed her into the dining room.

'You're as bad as Jack,' scolded Aunty Meg fondly. 'He was totally incorrigible when he was your age, and he hasn't changed all that much where cheekiness is concerned! Now, children, do sit down and help yourselves.'

'One would almost think you had known each other for years,' said Aunty Meg as the children ate a hearty meal and chattered about the JEACs. 'Now, if you've had enough to eat, why don't you go out and enjoy the fresh air? Oh – before I forget – we recycle and have a compost heap here, so please make sure any paper is thrown into the special box in each of your rooms.'

'Sure, Aunty Meg,' said Anu. 'Also, please let us know how you would like us to help you. We're used to chores, and would be glad to do anything you like.'

The others nodded in agreement.

'Thank you, dear,' said Aunty Meg. 'That's very thoughtful of you, but if you just keep your rooms tidy and look after yourselves, that would be more than enough.'

Anu groaned, and confessed sheepishly, 'I'll do my best, Aunty Meg, but though I start off very neatly, in no time at all my room looks like a cyclone has struck! But Gina's very neat and she'll help me!'

The others chuckled, and Nimal, who had taken a great fancy to the older lady, said, 'I'm very good at vacuuming, too, Aunty Meg. I'm never happier than when pushing it around, and I even take Gina for a ride now and then. I'm going to be a house husband when I grow up and spend my whole life vacuuming.'

'Put a sock in it, Nimal! The last time you vacuumed the place, Mum had to take you to hospital,' said Rohan with a grin. 'He was so busy vacuuming that he didn't notice the staircase behind him – he fell down the stairs and not only sprained his ankle but got a big cut on his head. And, Aunty Meg, I'm sure you've already noticed that Nimal doesn't *need* an excuse to trip over things or fall down!'

'Hey, big boy,' said Nimal, throwing a friendly punch at Rohan who ducked it, 'come on out and we'll have a karate fight!'

The six of them were chased out of the house by Aunty Meg who, after thanking Nimal for his kind offer, said that they could manage the vacuuming very well without him!

'Do you guys learn karate?' asked Amy enviously. 'I've been longing to learn but haven't had time. What levels have you reached?'

'Nimal's a blue belt and I'm a purple,' said Rohan. 'We've been learning for a while now, and it sure keeps you fit. The girls start next term.'

They wandered around the garden, chatting amicably. Anu had handed out JEAC badges and they all wore them proudly.

'Hey, there's Uncle Jack,' said Nimal, as he spotted Jack coming out of the house.

Gina and Mich ran to meet him, hanging on his arms.

'Did you just return, Uncle?' asked Rohan. 'What did the others say about that Ingram chap?'

'I'll tell you over my tea,' said Jack. 'Do you mind if we sit down for a bit? I'm rather bushed as it's been a hectic afternoon and quite hot.'

'Sit here,' said Amy quickly, drawing up a chair for him. 'We'll look after you.'

'Yes,' chorused the others and ran off to get him tea and sandwiches. He was soon well supplied with everything.

'I like your badges,' said Jack. 'And I see you Larkins have joined up, too. I was so glad when I heard about the JEACs. Helen wants to talk to you about it and then try and start a group here.'

'Sounds great, Uncle Jack,' said Anu.

'Now, I guess you want to know what happened at our staff meeting?' he said.

'Yes, please,' said Nimal eagerly.

Jack told them what had been discussed and concluded by saying, 'Well, we've taken some preventative measures for the time being. We've hired more security guards to patrol the area and the staff have been alerted to look out for anything suspicious, but until we hear from Ingram or Owen, or something happens, we really can't do much more. However,' he continued, getting up from his seat, 'let's forget about them. The tea has revived me. Who wants to go for a boat ride?'

'Me! Me!' they chorused, following him down to the boat and clambering into it.

Jack started the engine, Rohan untied the boat from its moorings, and they were off!

'We'll go up river first,' said Jack, 'and you can see the source, and then we'll go down river till we come to where it meets the sea.'

'Great,' said the boys, who were busy examining the boat.

'That's a powerful motor you have, Uncle Jack,' said Rohan.

'Yes, it's a 200-horsepower motor,' said Jack, adding with a laugh, 'but if you want technical details, please ask Okanu.'

Gina suddenly burst into song and everyone listened to her lilting voice as she changed the words to a well-known song.

'Way down the Moosanagi River, far, far away
Out in the Gold Coast of Australia,
That's where our Uncle Jack stays.
Everywhere you turn there's beauty,
There'll be dolphins, too,
We know that we will have a great time,
'Cause there is tons to do.'

The others burst out laughing and clapped at Gina's little song. She looked around with a grin and said, 'Come on, join in.'

They did so enthusiastically, and as Jack and Mich could sing in harmony and the others all sang well, people turned their heads to smile at the happy crowd in the boat, waving to them as they went by.

'Did you make that up on the spot, Gina?' asked Amy when they had stopped singing.

'Er – yes,' said Gina, turning pink.

'That's excellent, love,' said Jack. 'Have you made up any more songs?'

'Just nonsense verse,' admitted Gina shyly.

'She's very good,' said Anu, smiling at her sister. 'After dinner, if she doesn't mind, we'll ask her to recite one of her poems. And Mich,' she continued, 'I hear you're brilliant at drawing. Would you show us your cartoon book, too?'

'Oh!' said Mich, with a blush. 'Well, if Gina recites her poem, I don't mind showing you my cartoons.'

'Great,' said Jack who liked to encourage the children to share their talents. 'I think we're set for a good evening.'

'I can see mountains,' said Gina suddenly, pointing to the left.

'Is that where the source of the river is, Uncle?' said Amy.

'Yes – and it would take hours to reach it,' said Jack. 'Let's turn around now, but I'll stop for a few minutes, and Anu can take pictures.'

Anu took pictures of the mountain range, and of all the others, Rohan pretending to man the boat, and then Jack took a picture of all of them. Amy made sure she was standing next to Rohan, and Anu suppressed a grin as she noticed it.

'Okay! Now – towards the ocean we go!' said Jack, turning the boat. 'Would you boys like to take a turn at the wheel for a bit? It's a little too powerful for you girls, unfortunately, but you can try out the smaller motor boat at the Conservation.'

Of course the boys wanted to steer the boat! With Jack guiding them, they each took turns till they could see the ocean in the distance, and then Jack took over again.

'Are we going out to sea, Uncle?' asked Gina.

'Not tonight, hon. The water's rather choppy just now; but Okanu knows these waters better than I do, so he'll take you out one day. Have you gazed your fill? Shall we turn back?'

'Sure,' said Rohan, 'though I could stay on the boat forever. It's superb!'

'Gee, how time flies when we're having fun!' said Amy, looking at her watch. 'Can you beat it? It's nearly eight.'

'Aunty Meg will have my head on a platter if we're not back in time for dinner,' said Jack, immediately turning the boat around. 'Hang on, kids!'

He started the motor again and they flew up the river. The youngsters yelled with joy as the water sprayed them. It had been a hot day with temperatures in the thirties, and it was wonderful to feel the wind in their faces and the water cooling them down.

They got back in record time, and rushed in to tell Aunty Meg about their trip.

'And Gina made up a song, too, Aunty,' said Mich, who was becoming very talkative. 'Sing it for her, Gina.'

'You sing, too,' said Gina, and the two of them sang the song for Aunty Meg who thoroughly enjoyed it.

'Dinner in ten minutes,' said Aunty Meg, when they had finished singing, and they rushed upstairs to wash their hands and tidy up. The boat ride had tossed their hair, and Mich and Gina, with their curly hair, looked quite wild and windswept.

After dinner, everyone adjourned to the comfortable living room to relax before going up to bed. Anu was encouraged to be the narrator and give them a brief version of their summer adventure, while the other Patels and Mike took up the tale as requested. Mich's cartoons were much admired and each of the Patels promptly asked the little girl to draw them pictures. She was only too willing to do so. Gina recited one of her poems, and then it was bedtime.

'Now, JEACs, you have a busy day tomorrow and must be up early – Nimal, I heard that groan,' said Jack.

'What time?' asked Anu.

'6:30, please, downstairs – all set to go!' said Mike. 'That way we can eat breakfast and leave the house by 7:15 at the latest. Knowing Nimal, he'll die of hunger if we don't feed him first. I'll drop you off at Roma Street – your tour starts at nine, and believe you me, the Australians are very punctual – no "Indian standard time" here.'

The Patels and Jack laughed, and Mich asked, 'What's Indian standard time, Mike?'

'Sorry, Mich,' said Mike, 'It's a saying in India. Many Indians are very laid-back and have little or no sense of punctuality – if they're asked to be somewhere at nine, they could very easily arrive by eleven and nobody thinks it's strange!'

'Oh – thanks, Mike,' said Mich with a grin.

The youngsters said goodnight and trooped up to bed, Rohan agreeing to set his alarm and wake the others at 5:30.

The Larkin girls seemed quite as comfortable as the Patels to let Rohan take charge in certain areas and, since he was a born leader with the ability to empower others, the group functioned well.

As Amy said to Mich while they prepared for bed that night, 'You know, Mich, it's great to finally meet the Patels. The boys are really decent, Anu and Gina are adorable, and they're all such fun!'

'Yes,' agreed Mich, 'and it's so nice to have brothers, isn't it Amy?'

'Cool,' said Amy, turning away to hide a small smile. 'Now, go to sleep, chicken – tomorrow will be fun!'

The next morning everyone was ready before 6:30 and they rushed down to the dining room.

'Wow, you must have been up even earlier than us,' said Rohan, as they entered the room and saw most of the adults already getting up from the table.

'We've got an early start at work,' said Okanu with a smile.

'But – do you work on Saturdays?' asked Mich.

'Honey, for the time being, till the Conservation is up and running smoothly, we work every single day, and some nights, too,' said Czainski. 'Your Uncle Jack is a slave driver.'

'Where is he?' asked Nimal, sitting down with a plate of food.

'Oh, he left for work at five,' said Mike grinning at them. 'He's a real workaholic, that man. He says he wants to be able to spend time with you folk this evening and tomorrow.'

'Not that he leaves much later when you aren't around,' said Jalila, moving towards the door. 'He's usually at work by 6:30 in the morning and doesn't come back till nine or ten at night. Well, JEACs, have a lovely day, and we'll look forward to hearing about it tomorrow.'

'How did you know we were called the JEACs?' asked Gina in surprise. 'We're not wearing our badges.'

'Oh – a little bird told us about it, Gina,' said Padmini, winking at Mike.

'Not that little!' said Mike with a grin. 'All of us heard about the JEACs at a staff meeting when Jack read out Anu's email – and they were thrilled! I'll see you in a bit,' he continued, waving a piece of toast at the others as they left the room.

The youngsters waved, too, and quickly finished breakfast. They were excited at going on a tour, and were soon loaded into the Land Rover, waving goodbye to Aunty Meg as they drove off.

CHAPTER 6

Lots of Fun – and a Horrid Experience

'Wow! What a gorgeous country, Mike!' exclaimed Anu, looking around as Mike drove along the highway to the city. 'It was too dark to see anything when we arrived.'

'It is beautiful,' agreed Mike, 'Also, as Brisbane doesn't have a severe winter, everything stays green throughout the year.'

Half an hour later they were driving up the ramp to the Roma Street bus station. There were several vanloads of people getting off at the station, and Mike explained that hotels all around the city made arrangements for those of their guests who wanted to go on tours, dropping them off at the bus station.

'It's very well organized,' said Mike, 'and the tour guides know many stories and anecdotes about the country.'

Mike gave Rohan enough money for expenses and emergencies, made sure he had the mobile phone, and then ushered them into the bus station.

'Right, folks,' said Mike, 'here are your tickets and a red sticker for each of you to put on your shirts. Should I give all the tickets to Rohan?'

'Yes, please,' said Amy, 'if Rohan doesn't mind.'

'No problemo!' said Rohan. 'Mike, I noticed that people are wearing different-coloured stickers. Is that because they're on other buses?'

'No – you'll see people in your bus wearing different colours, too,' said Mike. 'Some people are booked for only two or three stops, while others just want to go to one place and spend a long time there – and the stickers help the driver identify the groups. Right! I'll be back at five to pick you up. Have a lovely time and stay safe.'

'Thanks a ton, Mike!' said the youngsters, waving to him as he drove off.

They were quite early, so they purchased some postcards and sent them off to their parents, Bindu and a few friends in India and Canada.

With ten minutes to go, they wandered outside, watching the different buses load up with people going on various tours.

'G'dai, maites! Owyagoin'?' said a hearty voice behind them. They turned around, and the man continued, 'And what 'ave we 'ere? The "Sensational Six" I dew b'lieve! You are all on me tour, as I can tell from your stickers! Me name's Ralph, and as you can see, though vertically challenged, me 'eart's in the roight place!'

The children couldn't help laughing as he shook hands with each of them. He was an enormous Australian, well over six feet tall and very broad. He had twinkling blue eyes in a square, tanned face, and sported a handsome moustache and a perpetual grin.

'Right – now, me lad, you look like the biggest of the lot. Did they trust you with the tickets?'

Rohan handed them over.

'Goodonya,' said Ralph, opening the door of the bus and ushering them in.

Nimal got in last, tripping over the step as usual, and of course Ralph teased him about it.

'That step keeps disappearing and reappearing, lad,' he said, 'especially when folks like you are around.

'Now, perhaps you girls could sit in the front seats so you have a great view through the windscreen,' he continued, poking his head into the bus. 'And, since you lads are taller, you can sit behind them and look over their heads.'

They agreed to his seating arrangements and settled themselves comfortably. Ralph greeted other tourists as they came up to the bus and soon everyone was seated and raring to go.

'All aboard!' sang out Ralph, climbing into the driver's seat and closing the door. 'Well, ladies and gen'lemen we're off – not to see the Wizard of Oz – but to see some of Brisbane, God's own country!'

He was extremely entertaining and kept everyone in fits of laughter. He was also a born storyteller and it was clear that he loved his job and knew the country well.

'First stop, Busy Bee Farm,' sang out Ralph, turning off the highway an hour later. 'All those with red and yellow stickers get off here and I'll be back in an hour. Those with blue and green stickers, please stick on the bus, and I'll drop you off at the sanctuary.'

The children got out.

'Watch out for that disappearing step, maite,' said Ralph, as Nimal climbed down. 'See you later, gang.'

They went towards the building and read the sign held up by a large model of a bee which said, 'G'day. Come inside and watch all m'little mates working flat out for Australia at the Busy Bee Farm.'

'Sounds interesting,' said Nimal, leading the way in.

The guided tour was highly educational. Back in the souvenir shop they tasted the different brands of honey, also used for medicinal purposes, and picked up a few gifts.

Soon they were back on the bus and Ralph drove them to the Glenforest Sanctuary.

'This is a fabulous sanctuary,' said Ralph. 'They have mainly deer, emus, wallabies, kangaroos and koalas. You can, if you wish, have your picture taken as you cuddle a koala. However, for those who wish to cuddle me instead, I assure you I don't bite – whereas the koalas may!'

'We'd sure like a picture of you cuddling all of us,' said Amy promptly.

'No worries! See you red stickers in an hour an' a half,' said Ralph.

Only the children got out at the sanctuary where they were greeted by another Australian.

'Owyagoin', mates – I'm James. Welcome to the Glenforest Sanctuary. I'll be taking you to see the koalas first, and then on a tractor ride to see the other animals. Follow me.'

He was a fascinating guide and gave them innumerable details about the functioning of the sanctuary, especially when he learned that they lived on conservations themselves.

'This is great!' said James enthusiastically. 'I've met Jim Patel and Chris Larkin – and who in the conservation world doesn't know Jack and admire his ideas on conservation. I certainly wish him all the best in his new venture.'

The children were thrilled with the koalas, especially when James showed them the newest baby who was just six months old. 'Some people call them koala *bears*,' said James, 'but that's incorrect. Koalas are marsupials – animals that carry their young in a pouch, like kangaroos. Watch this baby trying to creep into her mother's pouch again. Notice that the koala's pouch opens up from below – unlike the kangaroo's – and babies climb up and cling on tight.'

The ride in the tractor was superb. James gave each JEAC a bucket of food for the animals. Whenever the tractor stopped, the animals would come up for food and, of course, they crowded around Nimal, trusting him instinctively. James and the Larkins were amazed at the way the creatures nuzzled the boy.

They finally had to say a reluctant goodbye to James, thanking him for the wonderful tour. He promised to keep in touch and told them he would be attending the special opening day of the new Conservation.

'All aboard once more,' called out Ralph, who was waiting for them. 'Next stop, the Big Pineapple, and food! Are you folks hungry by now?'

'You bet!' said Nimal, Gina and Mich.

'I was just wondering if we were *ever* going to eat again,' said Gina.

'But if you eat too much you'll get fat, me darlin',' said Ralph, smiling at the little girl who was as thin as a rake.

The bus meandered its way through the beautiful countryside.

'Oooh!' squealed Mich a little later, 'look at that simply gigantic pineapple!'

'That's how the farm gets its name, hon,' said Ralph, turning into the driveway. 'It's a pineapple farm. You can eat lunch, go on a train ride and learn about pineapple farming, visit the miniature zoo and feed the animals.'

He stopped the bus and reminded everyone that he would be setting off again in a couple of hours. The children asked him to take a picture of them in front of the big pineapple, which was about 9.1 metres high. He took the photograph, and then they asked one of the others on the tour to take a picture of all of them with Ralph.

Ralph departed to deal with official business and the children went in search of something to eat.

The restaurant was serving a wonderful buffet lunch, and the JEACs were soon eating hungrily, chatting about all they had seen.

'I'm so glad Uncle Jack sent us on this tour,' said Anu. 'It's simply fantastic.'

'It's superfantabulous,' said Nimal. 'There are a lot of conservations in Brisbane. Wasn't it neat finding out that James knew our parents?'

'Sure was,' said Rohan. 'What's the name of the conservation your parents manage, Amy? I know Uncle Jack's mentioned it, but I can never remember the name, sorry – it sounds very "Eskimo", if you know what I mean.'

'Manipau Wildlife Conservation Centre,' said Amy. 'Actually, my parents made up the name – it sounds Inuit, but isn't really. The way we remembered it when we were younger was to think of *many paws*.'

'Great word association,' said Anu. 'I don't think I'll ever forget the name now.'

The others laughed and agreed with her.

'What's "Inuit"?' asked Gina.

'They're the members of indigenous tribes living in northern Canada, Greenland and Alaska,' explained Amy. 'They used to be called Eskimos – but it's politically correct to call them Inuit.'

'Wow, have you actually *seen* Inuits?' asked Gina.

'We have Inuits living and working on the Conservation.'

'Oh, gosh – sorry to interrupt, folks, but just look at the time!' exclaimed Rohan, glancing at his watch. 'It's nearly 1:30 and Ralph will be back for us in an hour. Has everyone finished?'

'Gee whizz! I can't believe we've already been here an hour,' said Amy. 'It's all your fault, Nimal,' she teased, 'you kept forcing us to take second and third helpings of food – just to keep you company.'

'Huh! Are you on my case, too?' growled Nimal. 'Bad enough I have three people who complain about my appetite, and now you start. I guess Mich will be next. This is definitely one of the saddest stories of my life!'

Laughing as they left the restaurant, they saw the tiny train station.

'It's getting ready to go,' said Amy. 'C'mon – run!'

The driver saw them coming, waited until they had scrambled into the little carriages, and set off, describing enthusiastically how pineapples were cultivated and picked. At the end of the ride, he dropped them off at the miniature zoo.

They had fun feeding the animals – the kangaroos were so tame they would come up and eat out of their hands, and each child had a photograph taken of them feeding the kangaroos. They would make lovely souvenirs.

They went back to the big pineapple structure and Mich wanted to go to the bathroom, so Amy accompanied her.

The Patels wandered around, admiring the scenery. As Amy and Mich were returning to join the Patels, a teenage boy accosted them.

'Hi there, cutie,' he said, leering at Amy. 'I'm Don, and this is my mate, George. We're here on our own – are you with your parents?'

Amy took an instant dislike to Don. 'We're with a group of friends,' she said coldly, taking Mich's hand and walking on.

'Hold on, sweetie,' said Don moving into her pathway and forcing her to stop. 'What's the rush? We're here in our car, why don't you join us? Who're your friends anyway?'

'They're over there,' said Amy, pointing to the Patels, who were not looking in their direction. Rohan and Nimal were seated on a bench watching Anu taking pictures of Gina posing in front of the big pineapple.

'You mean you're with that group?' said Don insolently. 'Surely not. They're just scum. Leave your kid sister with them and you and I can cuddle up.'

Amy lost her temper. Quick-tempered at the best of times, when people made derogatory remarks about others, whether they were her friends or not, her temper flared.

'You *moron*!' she said angrily. 'It's people like you who give us a bad name for being discriminatory. Now, get out of our way before I yell for our friends to come and deal with you.'

Don sneered nastily and snapped, 'Sure, call them and see what happens. I'm a karate champ. They won't have the guts to come over.'

Mich burst into tears. 'Rohan! Nimal!' she yelled.

'Trouble,' snapped Rohan, hearing panic in the little girl's voice.

He and Nimal raced over to where the Larkins were standing, their way still blocked by Don and George. Anu and Gina quickly followed the boys.

'You okay, Amy?' asked Rohan. He rapidly sized up Don and George.

'No,' said Amy through her teeth, 'these two morons are blocking our way.'

'Please step aside so that our friends can join us,' said Rohan politely.

Don and George had taken stock of the boys, too. Rohan's height and muscles were obviously not to be underestimated, and Nimal, standing beside Rohan with his hands clenched, looked an equally tough customer.

'Who asked you to interfere?' said Don belligerently. 'We aren't scared of *#@%$ like you – take a hike – you're polluting the air around me!'

Before Rohan or Nimal could say a word, there was a loud *smack* as Amy, losing her cool completely, slapped Don across the face with all her strength, leaving an imprint of her hand on his face.

'How *dare* you?' she said, her voice trembling with anger. 'You, you . . .' She choked, tears of rage pouring down her cheeks.

'You little *!%,' said Don viciously, raising his arm to hit her back.

'Enough,' growled Rohan angrily, stepping in front of Don and grabbing his arm. 'You asked for it, dude,' he continued, 'and if you don't get lost right now, you'll be begging for trouble from us.'

Don felt the power in Rohan's grip and knew that he was no match for the boy. He wrenched his arm away from Rohan and backed away from the children.

'You're garbage,' he yelled, and spat at Rohan's feet. Then, scared at the looks of fury on the boys' faces, he and George made a run for their car.

Rohan and Nimal turned to give chase, but Anu swiftly grabbed them by their arms.

'No!' she said sharply, more to Rohan than to Nimal. 'Cool it – you know it's not worth mixing with them.'

The boys stared at her for a moment, both of them rigid with anger.

'Okay, Anu – you're right,' said Rohan, trying to calm down, while Nimal punched the air in frustration. 'You can let go of me now, sis,' he continued with a forced grin as Anu still hung on.

'Don't cry, Mich,' said Gina, hugging her, while tears of empathy ran down her face.

'They're a couple of jerks!' said Rohan, putting his arm around Amy to give her a brief hug. 'Please don't cry, Amy – it's not worth it. What happened?'

Amy told them, and then continued, 'I'm so mad! I hate arrogant, chauvinistic guys like them.' She tried to control her anger and her tears. 'I'm sorry I nearly caused a fight,' she said remorsefully, 'but I couldn't stand the way he behaved. I'm not sorry I slapped his face, though – he deserved it, and more!'

They walked slowly to the driveway, ignoring Don and George who were in a car, watching to see where they went. They wanted to give the group a fright by driving the car at them, but fortunately Ralph arrived just then and his bus blocked the car. The frustrated boys had no option but to drive off, which they did slowly, shaking their fists angrily.

'Owyagoin', maites?' asked Ralph. Then he noticed their faces. 'What's up?' he asked.

'Just a problem with some troublemakers,' growled Nimal, pointing at the car which was still in sight. 'They're lucky Anu stopped us going after them – they'd have been in *major* trouble then. If Rohan had less self-control not even Anu could have stopped him from teaching them a lesson!'

'Huh – believe me, I'm having a tough time trying to stay cool, yaar,' said Rohan, gritting his teeth.

Ralph ushered them into the bus and Amy told him what had happened. He was livid!

'I'm sorry, maites,' Ralph apologized. 'I hope you won't let this spoil your trip.'

'We'll be okay,' said Amy, and the others nodded slowly.

'Goodonya,' said Ralph. 'Now, let me check up on the rest of the folk in this bus, and I'll be right back.'

He went off, returning shortly with ice creams for all of them, and though they told him they were fine, they were very appreciative of his kindness and generosity.

They set off for the Underwater World and Ralph succeeded in making them laugh so much that they forgot their nasty experience for the time being. It was wonderful to walk in the tunnel with hundreds of varieties of fish in all sizes, shapes and colours, swimming over and around them. They had a good time taking crazy pictures and emerged from the tunnel cheerfully.

Soon it was time to return to Roma Street bus station, and they got there at 5 p.m. They thanked Ralph for the lovely tour and told him they were going on a city tour the next day.

'Well, goodonya,' said Ralph grinning widely. 'Guess who'll be your guide tomorrow?'

'You?' cried Gina and Mich together.

'That's right, maites – on the button as usual,' said Ralph.

They said goodbye, glad they would see him again the next day.

'There's Mike's Land Rover,' said Nimal.

They clambered into the vehicle, chattering nineteen to the dozen as they told him about their day. They did not tell him about the experience with Don. Mike noticed that Amy was rather withdrawn, but as it had been a long day he assumed that she was just tired.

'Here we are,' said Mike, as they reached the house. 'I won't get out as I have to get back to work for a bit.'

'Is Uncle Jack back?' asked Amy.

'He should be in by seven,' said Mike. 'I know he wanted to tell you about his ideas for the Conservation, especially about the dolphins. I'll bring him back with me.'

The children went inside and Aunty Meg wanted to hear about their tour. 'Join me on the lawn when you are ready,' she said, as they all wanted to change; it had been a hot, sticky day.

As they went upstairs, the younger girls running ahead, Rohan said to the teens, 'Do you think we should tell Uncle Jack about what happened?'

'Of course,' said Amy promptly. 'The kiddies were very upset, too. What do you think, Anu?'

'Yeah, I guess,' said Anu thoughtfully. 'It would be good to talk to him and debrief, especially since Gina and Mich haven't been exposed to something like that before. Perhaps he can help us to deal with it and stop being so mad.'

'Right,' said Rohan, 'we'll discuss it after dinner. Will you bring it up, Amy?'

'Sure.'

Joining Aunty Meg on the lawn, they told her all about the tour and showed her the souvenirs they had bought. She enjoyed their chatter and thanked them for the bottle of honey they gave her.

'I can hear Mike's vehicle,' said Nimal.

They ran to greet Jack and Mike, and after dinner they moved into the living room.

'I'll organize something to drink,' said Aunty Meg, bustling away. 'And we can have dessert when we are ready for it.'

'Ah, good to be at home and have all of you around,' said Jack, relaxing in his favourite armchair.

Mike and Rohan carried in two trays with tea, coffee and hot chocolate, and everyone helped themselves.

The children stretched out on the thick carpet and then, Amy, looking rather serious, told Jack about the incident with Don.

'I'm sorry I lost my temper, but I'm not sorry that I whacked him. Why on earth are there people like him in this world?' concluded Amy angrily.

Not one of the adults said a word, and Mike rose jerkily from his chair and walked over to look out of the window, his fists clenched in anger. Mike, normally a peaceful and good-humoured man, had a temper that folk rarely saw. But let anyone harm animals or behave in a nasty manner, and he could become quite dangerously angry.

Jack sat rigidly in his chair, his hands gripping the arms so tightly that the children saw the blood drain out of them; a pulse beat rapidly in his jaw and it was clear that he was as mad as fire.

Aunty Meg had tears in her eyes and was the first to break the silence as she said in her soft voice, 'My dears, I am so sorry you had this nasty experience. What can we do about it, Jack?'

Jack took a deep breath, called Mike to join them, and said, 'Okay, kids – let's debrief and deal with this so that we don't destroy ourselves by hanging on to our anger.'

Jack led the discussion, encouraging the teens to use simple language so that the younger girls could understand easily.

After half an hour of everyone venting and expressing their views, Jack drew the discussion to a close. 'So – negative attitudes exist all over the world and though we don't have to necessarily use physical strength to fight it, sometimes that's the only way to deal with jerks,' he said.

'And we have a choice!' continued Jack. 'We can choose to let this kind of behaviour upset us for the rest of the evening, or weekend – *or* – we can choose to be more aware of our own behaviour which may upset others, learn from this experience and then let go of the bad feelings. What do you want to do?'

'Definitely the latter!' chorused the JEACs.

Jack was satisfied.

'Now,' he said with a cheery smile, 'Aunty Meg, do you think that we could have our dessert?'

'Of course, dear,' she said. 'Anu and Amy, could you help me dish out? And Mike and Rohan, would you bring in the dessert plates and forks from the dining room, please, and the big bowl on the side table.'

'What's for dessert, Aunty Meg?' asked Nimal.

'Pavlova,' said Aunty Meg.

'What's that?' asked Mich.

'One of our favourite Aussie desserts,' explained Aunty Meg. 'It's named after the famous Russian ballerina, Anna Pavlova. It has a meringue shell which is filled with fruit and whipped cream.'

'Mmmm – looks yummy,' said Gina, as Mike brought in the dish.

Soon each of them had a large helping of pavlova and they settled down to enjoy it.

When they were satiated and the plates had been cleared away, Rohan said, 'Tell us about the Conservation, Uncle Jack – we don't even know its name yet.'

CHAPTER 7

A New Concept and More Sightseeing

'Aquatic Fantasia Conservation and Dolphin Bay', said Jack. 'We have the signboard up already – hmmm, where shall I start?'

'With your idea about the dolphins,' said Mike, enthusiastically. 'It's a brainwave! Tell them the whole story, Jack.'

'Well, as you know, I wanted to open a conservation especially for sea creatures, so that people could not only see them but also learn about them in a positive atmosphere,' began Jack.

He was a great storyteller, and the JEACs listened in fascination.

'Dolphins have been around for 30 to 40 million years, compared to our one million or so, and are mentally, emotionally and socially very highly developed. They have an exuberant joy in being alive and are always smiling and dancing. It's been shown, scientifically, that they have a larger brain than humans and have greatly evolved emotions. They're compassionate, humorous and live in perfect harmony within large social groups.

'Particularly fascinating were all the stories I heard about the way in which these marvellous creatures reached out to humans – not only helping them when in trouble, like saving drowning people, but also seeking them out to play with. There are countless such stories, but I will tell you only one for now – repeated to me by a friend – about a woman in Monkey Mia, a place here in Australia.

'One full moon night this woman couldn't sleep so she went out on the deck and found a dolphin splashing around. She took some fresh fish from her cooler and offered it to the dolphin, who took it, smiling as usual, right from her hand. And now, over 60,000 people go there every year;

they stand in shallow water to feed, stroke and play with over a dozen dolphins who have chosen to reach out to humans.

'We also learned that it was not fair to keep dolphins in captivity, no matter how much they loved us and we loved them. They were not free to be themselves when confined in man-made pools, and often died earlier than they would in their natural habitat.

'So I decided that I would try and encourage people to learn more about dolphin conservation by *inviting* dolphins to interact with us rather than forcing them to do so. Our Conservation has a bay that is perfect for my dream! The seabed slopes gently down from the beach and reaches a depth of twelve metres within the bay. Two "arms" of land enclose the bay with a twenty-metre gap between the tips. The arms are quite wide, and we've built a high fence right along the arms on both sides, to prevent anyone falling into the sea which is much deeper just outside the bay. We've also built tiered seats, back to back, one set facing the bay and the other facing the open sea, so that people can watch the dolphins play in the bay, and then watch them diving and playing in the open sea. The dolphins will not be controlled or restrained in any way, and will be free to come and go as they choose.

'And those are just the basics of what we are attempting to accomplish,' concluded Jack.

'Awesome!' said Nimal passionately. 'What an absolutely superfantabulous idea, Uncle Jack.'

'Gee whizz! It fits in with all I've read about dolphins and human psychology,' said Amy.

The youngsters were thrilled with the concept and eager to hear more. They peppered Jack and Mike with questions.

'But how will you find dolphins that want to come and interact with humans in your bay?' asked Rohan. 'And if you plan to have shows, won't you need to "invite" the dolphins to come into the bay at certain times, and how will they know?'

'They are the most intelligent creatures in the world,' said Mike. 'After one of Jack's fundraising campaigns, where he talked about his idea to a large group of conservationists, he was approached by a team who have been "communing" with a dolphin heptad.'

'What's a heptad?' asked Gina and Mich.

'It means *a group of seven*,' explained Jack. 'These people have been interacting with the heptad – on a daily basis – for five years – and can communicate with them beautifully. They have been asked, on numerous occasions, to bring their heptad into various conservations, but have refused because they didn't want their friends to be placed in captivity.'

'However, they loved Jack's idea, felt it would work beautifully, and for the past five weeks they've been at our Conservation,' said Mike.

'The dolphins come into the bay to play with them every day, at 10:30 in the morning, one in the afternoon, and five in the evening,' continued Jack. 'It's fascinating and heart-warming to hear the dolphins whistle and click as they communicate with each other and the group of humans. Those folk can ask them to do almost *anything*!'

'All I need, to make me feel at peace with the world after a rough day, is to see their smiling faces and watch them play,' said Mike. 'They're so much more *humane* than humans, if you know what I mean, and you can *feel* them reaching out to comfort you and cheer you up.'

There were lots more questions, mainly about the dolphins, and then it was bedtime.

'Tomorrow you don't need to get up too early,' said Mike. 'If you're ready by nine, I'll pick you up and drop you off at Roma Street. So have a good night, folks.'

The JEACs said goodnight and trooped off to bed. Tired out with the day's adventures, they fell asleep quickly, all of them dreaming of dolphins and making friends with them. Thanks to the debriefing with the adults, their nasty experience at the Big Pineapple was dealt with and let go.

Sunday dawned brightly and Nimal woke up at six. He looked over at Rohan, who was still fast asleep, and decided not to disturb him. He rose quietly, showered and dressed; then he ran downstairs and discovered Aunty Meg already in the living room, drinking a cup of coffee.

'You're up early, Nimal,' she said, smiling at the boy. 'Couldn't you sleep?'

'Good morning, Aunty Meg – no, I slept like a log, thanks. How are you?' said Nimal, and seeing that she had finished her coffee, he took her cup and placed it on the table.

'Thank you, love. I'm fine, just fine,' she said cheerfully. 'Would you like something to munch? I am sure you are "just starving"!' Her eyes twinkled as she quoted his favourite phrase.

'Actually, I am a tad peckish,' admitted Nimal with a grin, 'but I don't want to bother you. I'll get something if you tell me where to find it.'

'Well, Jack and Mike were off early, and had breakfast before they left. So, if you want some breakfast, you will find it in the dining room,' said Aunty Meg.

'You're a lifesaver, Aunty Meg,' said Nimal, giving her an impulsive hug. 'I would love an early serving of breakfast. Why don't you join me?'

'I'll sit with you for a bit, dear,' said Aunty Meg, 'but then I have things to do.'

Nimal got himself some food and amused Aunty Meg with tales of tricks he had played in school.

'Now, what are you going to do till the others come down?' asked Aunty Meg when Nimal had finished eating.

'Could I use the computer and check out some info on dolphins?' asked Nimal.

'Of course you can,' said Aunty Meg. 'The computer is in the little room off the library.'

Nimal got on the Net and downloaded masses of intriguing information about dolphins. He was absolutely fascinated by these amazing creatures. In no time at all it was 8:30. He heard the others coming downstairs and then Aunty Meg was calling to him.

'I'll be out in a jiffy, Aunty Meg,' he replied. He logged off and joined the others in the dining room.

'What, turning over a new leaf? You *never* get up so early – are you ill? I bet I know why you came down – you smelt bacon and eggs and wanted a head start on us.'

He grinned at the teasing and winked at Aunty Meg. 'Of course I didn't want extra brekker. I'm actually trying to lose a bit of weight because Aunty Meg says I'm too fat!'

The others chuckled as they sat down to eat a quick breakfast.

'I can see why you want to work with dolphins, Amy,' said Nimal. 'I was on the Net just now, reading up more about them, and they're really cool! I'm seriously going to consider joining Uncle Jack.'

'That's great, Nimal,' said Amy enthusiastically. 'I'm so looking forward to visiting the Conservation tomorrow to see them.'

'So are we,' chorused the others.

Mike arrived on the dot of nine, and the JEACs quickly piled into the Land Rover, with Rohan and Nimal in front.

'We collect Hunter tonight,' said Gina. 'We haven't seen him for ages and I really miss him. He'll like you and Amy, too, Mich.'

'Yeah,' said Nimal, 'and it'll be interesting to see which lady he tries to palaver this time.'

'Why?' asked Amy curiously, leaning over the seat to talk to him. 'Does he do any tricks?'

'Wait and see,' said Rohan mysteriously. 'He's a dog of many charms – after all, he belongs to us!'

'Well, if he's as charming as *you*,' said Amy, tweaking his hair, 'I'm sure we won't like him in the least!'

'Now, that's what I like to see, Amy,' said Nimal with a grin. 'Rohan put in place. Usually, as you can see, he bullies us, and we, being petrified, take it like lambs!'

'Would you like to stay *in* the car, Nimal, or would you prefer to run behind it?' growled Rohan, pretending he was going to open the door and push Nimal out.

'Peace, JEACs!' laughed Mike. 'It's good to hear your nonsensical conversations again. I sure missed it till I joined up with Jack and the gang.'

'Wow! We've reached our destination already,' said Anu, as they drove into the bus station a few minutes later.

'The programme for today is a tour of the city from nine to noon. They'll drop you off at the South Bank where there are lots of restaurants and shops – yes, Anu, bookshops, too!' said Mike, handing over some money to Rohan. 'After lunch, get directions to where the City Catamaran starts – it's also called the "City Cat". I suggest that you buy day passes and take a nice long ride in it, from one end of the city to the other. Meet us back at South Bank, in front of the Riverside Restaurant, at five and we'll go back to the Gold Coast for an early dinner and then pick up Hunter. All clear?'

They nodded and he waved goodbye to them and drove off. They were soon saying 'owyagoin', mate' to Ralph, who welcomed them back heartily.

'So, all set for another wonder tour with the handsomest chap in the world?' asked Ralph, twirling his moustache and winking at the children.

'Of course,' said Amy promptly. 'Where are you taking us today? To your house in Hollywood?'

'Now, now, luv,' said Ralph with a grin, 'don't get too cheeky! I may decide that we're definitely going to Hollywood – by bus. And then you'll be in trouble, because this bus – clever as she is – can't swim, but is extremely efficient at drowning.'

Carrying on in this vein, the children and the others going on the tour were soon on board the bus and driving out of the bus station. Brisbane was a beautiful city with a mixture of new and old buildings and beautifully kept gardens, and Ralph had interesting anecdotes about the areas they visited. He took them to the Hamilton area, where the upper echelon of society lived, and pointed out houses that cost millions of dollars. They even went past the Ascot horse racetrack, modelled on the famous one in England.

At the end of the tour, when they had to get off at South Bank, they were very sorry to part from Ralph and exchanged addresses with him, promising to keep in touch.

After a meal they wandered out into the shopping arcade.

'Can we go to a bookshop first, so I can buy the latest Harry Potter?' asked Anu. 'Mum said it may be cheaper here than in India. I'm just longing to read it.'

'Me, too,' said Amy. 'I also want Potter. They were all sold out in Canada at the store I went to, and it was going to take three weeks for an order to come through.'

They entered the largest bookshop in the block, and picked up two copies of Potter. Then, with Nimal and Rohan literally dragging Anu away from all the other books she wanted to look at, they wandered among the music and souvenir shops.

'Time to find the City Cat, folks,' said Rohan, who was keeping an eye on the time. 'It's nearly 3 o'clock and Mike said it would take us about an hour and a half to cruise the river.'

'Let's ask at that tourist information counter,' said Nimal. 'They're sure to point us in the right direction.'

'At last! A *man* who doesn't mind asking for directions. Wonders will never cease,' said Anu, clasping her hands dramatically. 'Are you sure you're feeling okay, Nimal? You don't have a temperature or anything?'

'No, and I'm still just a *boy*,' said Nimal with a grin. 'Gotcha, Anu! Plus – you're not being PC.'

'*Touché*,' said Anu, linking her arm in his. 'Okay, come on, *boy*, let's find this "cat" we're supposed to ride.'

The man at the information booth was very helpful and not only gave them directions, but sold them the tickets, too. They set off and in five minutes reached their destination.

'It's the Brisbane River,' said Amy, 'the same one Ralph pointed out on our tour. Uncle Jack said the City Cat is used by a lot of folk travelling to and from work, and especially by students and tourists.'

'There's a great view of the city, too,' said Anu.'

'Here's the wharf,' said Nimal, 'and look, Gina and Mich, can you see that boat – the blue and white one coming towards us – that's the City Cat.'

'Why's it called a "cat"?' asked Mich. 'It doesn't look like a cat to me.'

'Well, its proper name is "catamaran", which means a large boat, but they've shortened the name to "cat" which is easier on the tongue,' said Nimal, not wanting to get too technical with the youngsters.

A friendly chap welcomed them onto the boat, and they went inside the large cabin where the captain of the boat checked their passes. There was seating both inside the cabin and out, and the youngsters opted to stand outside, in the front, holding on to the rails, feeling the wind on their faces and the refreshing spray from the water. It was superb and the view was spectacular.

Anu got some lovely snapshots and all too soon it was time to disembark at South Bank and wait for Jack and Mike.

'There they are,' said Mich. She and Gina ran towards them and were swung up onto their shoulders. The others came up and soon they were telling Mike and Jack all about the day's events as they piled into the vehicle and returned to the Gold Coast.

CHAPTER 8

Hunter and Plans

'Now for Hunter,' said Nimal. 'How far do we have to go to pick him up, Mike?'

'A ten-minute drive,' said Mike. 'I'm longing to see the old fellow again.'

The Patels were excited – they had missed Hunter and his funny, affectionate habits.

'Perhaps Mike should go and get him,' suggested Jack, pulling into the driveway of the Veterinary Hospital. 'He has all the paperwork and the signing authority, since Hunter was sent to him.'

'Cool,' said the Patels.

After five minutes, Mike came back with Hunter, the dog jumping up at him and whining with pleasure at seeing him again. Then he spotted the children.

With one bound, Hunter flung himself at the Patels, barking happily, and it was a licky, sticky reunion! The Patels could not hug and pet Hunter enough, and the dog was so overjoyed to see them that he couldn't stand still for a minute. He recognized Jack and washed his face, too.

'Hunter, sit!' said Nimal after a few minutes. 'Shake with two friends.' He pointed to Amy and Mich.

To Mich's amazement, Hunter immediately sat down in front of her and waved his right paw in the air. She took it a bit nervously at first, but once she had shaken his paw and had her hand licked, she felt brave enough to pet the lovely dog. Hunter showed off his manners with Amy, too.

'What a lovable dog you are, Hunter,' said Amy, giving him a hug and getting her face washed in return. 'Oh, you Patels are so lucky to have him.'

Hunter was thrilled to be with his family again. He had a perpetual grin on his face and kept giving little wriggles and whines of joy, licking the children at every opportunity.

They drove home, following the Moosanagi, the children admiring the beautiful houses along the banks of the river.

'Uncle Jack, is it very expensive to buy a house on the riverbank?' asked Amy.

'It sure is – at least a million dollars,' said Jack with a chuckle.

'Man, there must be lots of rich people in the Gold Coast,' said Nimal in awe.

'Actually, they aren't necessarily rich,' said Mike. 'I heard an interesting story from a taxi driver when I first came here, and Czainski confirmed it. There's a particular group who do fundraising for various causes. They sell raffle tickets, five dollars each, to millions of people all over Australia, through outlets such as shopping malls and stores. If you're lucky, you could win a million dollar house!'

'Gee, that's incredible,' said Amy. 'So, you mean to say that all these houses have been won? Including yours, Uncle Jack?'

'Well, actually, no. I was unfortunately – or fortunately – one of those who paid for my house before the government gave the fundraisers the okay to run their scheme. There are a few of us old-timers. If you look carefully, you'll see that some properties, like mine, are about three times the size of others.'

'People go crazy over the tickets,' said Mike, 'because if you buy one ticket you get the house, completely fitted out; if you buy four tickets, you get a boat thrown in – and there are various other deals.'

'Can't we all buy tickets, Uncle Jack?' asked Gina. 'Then, if we win, we can live here!'

The others laughed at her, though they admitted the idea was appealing.

'Hey, look – that blue car – aren't those the two jerks we met at the Big Pineapple?' asked Rohan, who was looking out of the window while they stopped at a traffic light.

Everyone craned to look out of Rohan's window. The blue car was in the next lane, a wee bit behind their own.

'They sure are,' said Amy, grimacing, 'I'd recognize that moronic Don anywhere!'

'Perhaps they live around here,' said Mike, as the lights changed and they moved on. 'Well, you folk will be busy on the Conservation so, hopefully, you won't bump into them.'

'We'll keep our fingers crossed,' said Mich and Gina, simultaneously.

They reached home to find Aunty Meg already seated in the front garden. She had organized chairs and a table loaded with drinks and desserts and – was it true? Yes, it was indeed – a sumptuous chocolate cake!

'Aunty Meg, we got Hunter,' shrieked Gina, running to give her a hug, Mich close behind her.

'And he's absolutely sweet,' yelled Mich.

'Where is he?' asked Aunty Meg, smiling at the two exuberant little girls.

'He's right behind us,' said Gina, 'at least he was a minute ago,' she said, looking around for the dog who was nowhere to be seen.

The others came up and flopped down on the chairs and the grass.

'Where's Nimal?' asked Aunty Meg. 'Did you lose him on the tour?'

'Unfortunately, we didn't manage that,' said Anu with a grin. 'He said he wants to introduce Hunter to you in a very special way but had to make sure none of your flower beds were destroyed.'

As the Larkins looked mystified, Nimal strolled over from the back of the house, Hunter at his heels.

'Hunter, shake with a very special friend,' said Nimal.

Hunter sat down in front of Aunty Meg and waved his right paw in the air, and she shook it solemnly. Then he got up, ran to the back of the house, and a minute later, came back with a flower in his mouth, sat down again in front of her, and with a small whine, offered her the flower.

The others burst out laughing, though Aunty Meg was so impressed that she hugged the dog and immediately gave him a few biscuits from the table, which of course pleased Hunter enormously.

'Now, how did you get him to do that, Nimal?' asked Jack. 'I mean, he got flowers from the bush at the back of the house?'

'Well, I took him to the right bush, and introduced him to it,' said Nimal. 'I said, "Hunter, meet bush" . . . okay, okay,' he trailed off as the others threatened him, and continued with a grin. 'Being a very intelligent dog – Hunter, that is, not me – all I did was point at the bush and say "flower – YES". Then I took him over to a flower bed, pointed at it and said "NO", and he obviously cottoned on. I had a feeling he might want to give Aunty Meg a flower.'

'It's a trick he picked up before we had him,' explained Anu. 'He seems to think that any lady who is not a "girl" and who is introduced to him as "special" should be given a flower.'

'He's a lovely dog,' said Aunty Meg, watching as Hunter went around licking everyone. 'Now, where will he sleep tonight? With you children? I have no problem if you want him in your rooms.'

'You're a gem, Aunty,' said Nimal, going over to give her a bear hug. 'He usually sleeps on my bed, but he can sleep on the floor.'

'Oh, he can sleep on your bed, love,' said Aunty Meg, 'I don't mind that at all. My dog used to sleep on my bed, too, when I was growing up. Isn't he intelligent,' she continued, as Hunter came up to give her an extra lick. 'I am sure he understood what I said just now, and is thanking me.'

'He understands every word, Aunty,' said Gina immediately. 'He's a clever dog.'

They settled down on the lawn and had dessert. Of course Hunter got his share of doggie dessert, and – as Nimal teased Aunty Meg – the lion share at that!

They lazed around, enjoying the evening coolness and discussing dolphins and the Conservation. Okanu and Czainski joined them a little later, saying that Padmini and Jalila were too busy to return for dinner and that they themselves had to go back in an hour's time for meetings. Of course they were introduced to Hunter and fussed over him, too.

After they had heard about the children's day, Czainski turned to Jack and said, 'Something's cropped up with regard to the awareness campaign on Tuesday.'

'Problem?' asked Jack.

'Hmmm – potential,' said Czainski. 'I got a call from that chap, Ingram, about an hour ago. He wants to talk to you tonight about having a panel discussion with us at the campaign, so that he, Darrel and a couple of others can air their point of view.'

'He tried to tell Czainski that if we didn't agree to it, we were cowardly and unable to face opposition in public,' scoffed Okanu.

'Did he?' said Jack. 'And what did you say, Czainski?'

'I told him we were quite open to a panel discussion in public with them, and that once I had told you about it, you would be only too happy to accommodate him. I also reminded him that six months ago we tried to persuade him to have such a discussion, but he wasn't keen on it then. Guess he's changed his tune.'

'So we'll need to change the order of the programme once we've discussed this with Ingram tonight, and decide who'll be on our panel,' said Jack. 'I think four a side should be sufficient. Do we know who'll be on their panel?'

'Ingram, his nineteen-year-old son, who will represent the younger generation, and a couple of others from the lodge,' said Czainski. 'I think you should definitely be on the panel, Jack, and Helen, too. I also thought that perhaps Rohan could represent our younger generation, if he is willing to do so.'

'No problemo,' said Rohan.

'Good – we have a strong team, then,' said Jack. 'Now, about the fourth person on our team. Let's invite a guest from the public to join us at the event itself. That'll take Ingram and his team by surprise, and will give the public an opportunity to participate.'

'You mean, like a set-up, Uncle Jack?' asked Amy. 'Someone you'll choose ahead of time?'

'No, Amy,' said Jack. 'I mean a *real* guest with no previous warning – it'll make our stand even clearer.'

'Wow, that's fab!' said Anu.

'What about a moderator, Czainski?' asked Mike.

'I thought we should ask Judge Dickinson. Although he's an avid conservationist, being who he is, Ingram and crowd won't dare suggest he favoured anyone in the discussion. After all, the moderator just has to ensure that everyone gets a fair hearing – right?'

'Brilliant!' said Jack. 'Do you want me to ask him?'

Czainski nodded. Shortly after this Jack, Czainski and Okanu prepared to return to the Conservation.

'Mike,' said Jack, as he rose from his seat, 'please tell the JEACs about our plans for them.'

'Righto!' said Mike. 'Could one of you please ask Padmini to call me, and Helen, too? Thanks.'

He turned to the children.

'Well, JEACs, ready for hectic days? Lots of work for all of you – hope you don't mind.'

'Of course not, Mike,' said Rohan. 'Spill the beans.'

'Okay, tomorrow morning I'll take you to the Conservation. Helen will take charge from there on, and give you a rundown of the things she would like you all to do and participate in. And, no, I'm not saying anything more on that,' he said with a smile, as they immediately clamoured to know what he meant. He continued, 'At 10:30 you'll meet the dolphin heptad and their playmates. After that, around 12:30, Helen will give you some tasks which can be done at home, and I'll bring you back here for lunch.'

'Can't we lunch at the Conservation?' asked Nimal.

'Better yet, can't we live on the Conservation?' asked Amy. 'That would be so cool and we could do much more if we were staying there.'

'Well, since you've brought it up,' said Mike with a grin, 'we've already made plans for you to camp there – in tents.' He paused as they yelled with delight, and then continued, 'And, once tents, sleeping bags, and other paraphernalia have been organized, you'll be living on site – from Wednesday.'

'Cool,' said Rohan, 'and you'll give us lots to do, right?'

'Sure, yaar,' said Mike with a laugh. 'Why do you think we want you on site? We need the bathrooms cleaned, the whole place needs to be swept out daily, clothes have to be washed, and . . .' He broke off abruptly as the group, and Hunter, jumped on him, felling him to the lawn and tickling him till he begged for mercy.

'Peace, peace,' he cried, as he shook them off and sat up. 'Seriously, though – you'll have your hands full. Rohan, I know you're well aware of conservation issues, so we'll leave it to you to find out even more about sea creatures, especially dolphins, for the campaign on Tuesday; Helen will give you a briefing on the Conservation so you know where we're coming from. And now, if Hunter would be kind enough to stop using me as his own personal cushion, I have a lot of things to deal with.'

'Is there a schedule we can look at?' asked Anu. 'You know, just to get an idea of what's going on?'

'Yeah,' said Mike, as he rose from the grass and brushed himself down. 'Opening Day, or *OD* as we call it, is December twenty-second and Jack has a detailed schedule and timeline in the study. One of you can come with me and collect it.'

'I'll come,' said Anu.

'Meet us in the library, Anu. Do you mind us deserting you again, Aunty Meg? You're welcome to join us if you wish,' said Rohan politely, as they all went into the house.

'Thanks, Rohan,' said Aunty Meg, 'but I have many things I need to attend to.'

'I'll miss you terribly, Aunty Meg,' said Nimal, giving her another of his bear hugs.

'Get along with you, Nimal,' said Aunty Meg. 'I'll have a cracked rib in a moment! See you at bedtime, children.'

'Gee, this is so exciting,' said Mich. 'What kinds of things can we help with, Rohan?'

'Once we see the schedule we'll have a better idea, Mich,' said Rohan, smiling at the eager little girl. 'Ah – here's Anu with it.'

They pored over the large handwritten schedule. It was chock-a-block with information, but some items stood out in red ink and the children focused on those for a start.

'There's a full staff meeting every Monday morning,' said Anu, 'the awareness campaign is on Tuesday and the sky-train's scheduled for a test run on Thursday.'

'There's also a meeting in Jalila's office with all the actors,' continued Amy, 'and, gee, Anu, your name's down, too.'

'Mine?' asked Anu in surprise. 'Perhaps it's someone else with the same name.'

'No, it definitely says Anu Patel,' said Nimal. 'Perhaps they want you to write a play for one of the shows.'

'Oh – I'm sure it's not that!' said Anu.

'I bet I'm correct,' said Nimal. 'You *are* exceptionally good at writing.'

Rohan and Gina nodded in agreement and the Larkin girls looked duly impressed.

'Er . . . let's see what's next,' said Anu hurriedly, bending over the schedule once more. 'On Friday afternoon the dolphin playmates will be discussing their show, and then in the afternoon there's a meeting for all the waterskiers.'

'Gee, I didn't realize they'd have waterskiers, too – what fun!' said Amy.

'Amy's fantastic at waterskiing,' said Mich, looking at her sister proudly. 'She's won lots and lots of competitions.'

'Stop it, kiddo,' said Amy, turning red, 'you're making me blush.'

'Rohan's also very good at waterskiing, Amy,' piped in Gina. 'He won the prize at school. He also somersaults and jumps off high ramps.'

Both girls were happy that their older siblings were good at waterskiing.

'Now it's your turn to blush, Rohan,' ragged Nimal, as Rohan looked awkward. 'He's probably not as good as you, Amy, because he's only been doing it for a couple of years, but he's the best in our school.'

'Dry up, yaar,' growled Rohan. 'Now, let's see what else is going on,' he muttered, changing the topic.

Laughing, Anu looked at the schedule again. 'Well, everything appears to be work-related leading up to OD on the twenty-second,' she said.

They talked about the Conservation, dolphins and other sea creatures till an extra-wide yawn from Gina made Nimal look at his watch.

'Wow, look at the time! Bedtime, folks – it's ten and Mike said we'd need to be ready quite early tomorrow.'

'Ah, good, you have finished,' said Aunty Meg, coming into the library just then. 'Would any of you like a cup of something before you go to bed? Hot chocolate?'

'That would be terrific, Aunty Meg,' said Amy. 'Would you like some help?'

'No, thank you, dear. If you go upstairs and get ready for bed, I'll get someone to bring it to you. Goodnight and see you bright and early tomorrow.'

'Goodnight, Aunty Meg,' chorused the JEACs.

'Oh, I nearly forgot – Mike asked if Nimal and I could talk to him for a few minutes before we went to bed,' said Rohan to the others.

The boys went downstairs again.

The others finished their drink and tumbled into bed, excited at the prospect of finally going out to this Conservation they had heard so much about. They were especially looking forward to meeting the dolphins.

Gina and Mich fell asleep immediately, but Anu was restless. She finally got out of bed and peeped into the boys' room to see if they were awake.

'Come on in,' invited Rohan. 'Nimal palavered Aunty Meg into giving him some biscuits – want one?'

'Thanks,' said Anu, sitting down on Nimal's bed and nibbling her biscuit. 'I don't know why I can't fall asleep. I'm pretty tired, but my thoughts keep going round and round in my head, thinking about that Ingram chap. Do you think he'll cause problems at the campaign?'

'That's exactly what's bothering us,' said Nimal, joining Anu, 'and that's what Mike wanted to talk about. He's quite concerned about this chap – says he met him once and found he was a nasty piece of work. Mike asked us to keep our eyes skinned at the Conservation, and especially at the campaign, for any signs of trouble.'

'But what sort of trouble could they cause at the Centre?' asked Anu. 'I was thinking more about the campaign. Also, didn't Uncle Jack say they'd hired extra security guards to patrol the area?'

'Yeah,' said Rohan, 'but as Mike says, the Conservation is huge. Also, though the walls are high, the entrance to Dolphin Bay can't be walled in, and security guards can't be everywhere at once. Mike thinks it'll help when we're camped at the Centre. He and Uncle Jack will be staying there, too . . . come in,' he said, hearing a soft tap at the door.

'Thought I heard voices,' said Amy. 'I peeped into your room, Anu, because I just couldn't sleep, but you weren't there so I figured you must be here. Mind if I join you?'

'Of course not,' said Anu immediately.

Amy sat on the windowsill, stroking Hunter who had come up to greet her. 'I'm really worried about that horrible Ingram chap,' she began, and stopped when Rohan said with a grin, 'Join the crowd – that's just what we've been discussing.'

They told her about their discussion and Mike's request.

'What about the kids?' asked Amy. 'Do we tell them, or will it be too scary for them?'

'Oh, definitely tell them,' said Nimal promptly. 'Gina will hit the ceiling if we don't tell her, and she and Mich are very sharp. Who knows – they may spot some things quicker than we do simply because they're small and not that easily noticed.'

'True,' said Amy. 'Should we tell them in the morning?'

'Yeah, sure,' said Nimal, stifling a yawn and setting the others off. 'Boy, I think I'm finally ready for bed.'

The others nodded. The girls said goodnight and went to their rooms.

CHAPTER 9

Aquatic Fantasia Conservation and Dolphin Bay

All the youngsters were up before six – washed, dressed and down for breakfast in half an hour – surprising Aunty Meg, who had not expected any of them before seven.

'Good morning, JEACs,' she said. 'I am sorry but I don't have your breakfast ready yet. I just got rid of the adults. Are you starving or can you survive for half an hour?'

'I'm starving, Aunty Meg,' said Nimal, 'but because I love you to bits, I'll manage to survive till seven. By the way, where's Hunter disappeared to?'

'He's made friends with the cook, and is getting his breakfast in the kitchen,' said Aunty Meg, 'but I am sure that he will still join you for a second meal. He seems to take after someone else I know,' she added slyly, pretending to whack Nimal with a spoon as they left the dining room and went to the library.

'Gina and Mich,' said Rohan, 'listen up.' He told them about their concerns and concluded by saying, 'So we need to keep our eyes peeled. If you see *anything* unusual, or suspicious-looking people hanging around, let one of us know immediately – right?'

'Sure, Rohan,' said both children.

'Are we going to have another adventure?' asked Gina.

'Well, this whole trip is an adventure, Gina,' said Anu, 'but, hopefully, there won't be any danger this time.'

'Breakfast!' called Aunty Meg.

Hunter came out of the kitchen, licking his chops. He had been so well fed that he did not want anything more to eat – which was a first in a long time.

By the time Mike came to pick them up, the JEACs were raring to go. Hunter, sensing their excitement, joined in with little barks and whines, as they clambered into the Land Rover and drove to the Centre.

Within five minutes they were in the heart of the Gold Coast.

'And now,' said Mike, as they turned a corner, 'right ahead of you is the ocean.'

They saw the deep blue sea shimmering in the distance.

'Once OD is over, we'll take you surfing,' said Mike.

'Do you surf, Mike?' asked Amy.

'Not very well. I can stay on the surfboard, lying down, but can't stand up yet. I'll take a few lessons later on though, because it's fantastic, and I love the sea.'

A few minutes later, the vehicle turned right and they lost sight of the sea as they moved out of the main city into an area which was uninhabited except for a couple of small houses. They could see forestland a short distance from the road and the trees were a beautiful dark green.

'Hey – look! Ahead of us,' said Rohan suddenly. 'On the left.'

As they followed his pointing finger they saw a large sign, near an exit, which said 'Wilderness Adventures – 100 km'. There was a picture of a man with a gun, standing over a kangaroo which he had obviously just killed.

The children snorted in disgust as they read the sign.

'How much further do we have to go, Mike?' asked Anu. 'I thought we'd be following the ocean since the Conservation is for sea creatures, but at the moment, I feel like we're deep in the interior of the Gold Coast.'

'We're still fairly close to the ocean,' said Mike, 'and in about ten minutes, you'll see our Centre.'

Soon they were driving into an enormous car park, and though there were easily two hundred cars parked in it, it still looked empty.

'There's another parking lot on the other side,' said Mike, 'and next to it we have a special parking area for minivans and buses which bring in tour groups.'

'There's the sign,' said Gina happily, looking at the enormous board which formed an arch over the entrance to the Conservation. 'Aquatic Fantasia Conservation and Dolphin Bay', she read, 'and there's Uncle Jack!'

Jumping out, they ran to meet Jack.

'Welcome to our new venture,' said Jack. 'I'm sure you'll have a great time here.'

'We will, Uncle Jack!' they cried.

'Good – now, before we go in, let me tell you a bit about the site itself,' said Jack. 'The Conservation is situated on four square kilometres of land, and is only accessible by this main gate and by sea, via the bay – which is where the dolphins play. No one can enter it without permission.

At the entrance, as you can see, we have the gates and booths for ticket collectors, and there's a comprehensive information booth just inside the gates. We have staff residences – boarding houses and little chalets – and an area where staff and their families can relax during their free time.

As for the rest, I'll leave you to explore and discover things for yourselves. When you're free, you can go where you please. Everyone knows who you are – yes, you're notorious – and they've also heard about the JEACs – so don't be surprised if they greet you by that name. Now, let's go in!'

Jack ushered them through the entrance and into a large office close to it.

'Our offices are in this building,' said Jack, 'and these two are our front office representatives – Joe and Malika.'

'Hi, JEACs,' said Joe, shaking hands with them. 'I'm one of the receptionists and I'm a Canuck like you Larkin girls, but from Toronto.'

'I'm also a Canuck,' said Malika, greeting them in turn, 'but from a tiny place called Stouffville – just north of Toronto.'

'So what brought the two of you here?' asked Rohan curiously.

'I met Joey at school four years ago,' she paused, noticing Gina's puzzled look. 'In Canada we often call university "school",' she explained. 'We were both completing our environmental and conservation degrees – with a focus on sea creatures – in June this year, and were thinking about job prospects. One day Joey called me up and asked if I wanted a job in Australia. He had a friend, who had an aunt, who had a friend named Helen MacDonald, and Helen was looking for a couple of people who would not only be staff at this new Conservation, but who wanted the excitement of working with sea creatures and knew about conservation issues.'

'So, since we had naturally heard about Jack Larkin, and attended a few of his seminars when he visited Canada, and since we're both totally crazy about sea creatures, we thought we'd give it a shot and see if Helen would hire us,' said Joe.

'She did, and here we are,' said Malika. 'Australia's a great place, eh, Joe? It's absolutely stupendous to be in this environment with all the excitement and experience of the planning and hard work that goes into starting up a new conservation.'

'As you can tell,' said Jack, beaming at them, 'they just hate it here. By the way, they're more than receptionists, you know. They're the very first contact the outside world has with our Centre when they call or drop in – that's why we needed staff like them with excellent public relations skills. Now, let's find Helen.'

'Helen,' he yodelled, going into another office. 'Come out, come out, wherever you are. She's so tiny,' he continued, turning to the children, 'that often we can't see her behind her desk till she stands on it.'

They followed Jack into the office, wondering where this small lady was. Gina and Mich went round the desk to see if she was there, when a booming voice greeted them merrily from the doorway behind them.

'Hello there! You must be the JEACs. Jack, I heard you saying nasty things about my size again – and you'll pay for it.'

'It's tiny Helen!' chuckled Jack, delighted at the JEACs' astonishment as they gazed at Helen.

She was a massive lady – practically six feet tall! She had beautiful blonde hair, down to her shoulders, bright, twinkling blue eyes, and a beaming smile. She gave each of them, including Hunter, a hug.

'Welcome! I'm delighted to meet all of you,' she said warmly, petting the dog and bending double to do so. 'Jack, you can disappear now – I've had my fill of you,' she continued with a grin. 'And Czainski, Okanu and Jalila, not to mention thirty others, were all looking for you a while ago.'

'Help! What did they want?' asked Jack.

'I think they were interested in the idea of lynching you,' said Helen thoughtfully, 'but perhaps you'd better check with Monique.'

'Okay,' said Jack meekly. 'By the way, JEACs, as you know, Helen is our office manager and also co-ordinates our zillions of meetings – our office wouldn't function without her.'

'Thanks for the comps, Jack,' said Helen with a grin, 'but you won't worm yourself out of hot water that easily.' She turned to the group and continued, 'Monique is Jack's personal assistant in the office, and she also lives here – we share a chalet. Ah, there you are, Monique. Looking for Jack? Please take him away immediately and beat him up.'

'Bonjour, mes amis! It is great to finally meet all of you,' said Monique greeting each of the children with a kiss on both cheeks – she even kissed Hunter. 'I have heard so much about you from Mike and Jack. Mike talks about you, and Patiyak, incessantly, and has promised to take me to India one day.' She blushed slightly as she said this, but only Amy and Anu noticed.

She was a charming woman, in her late twenties, who barely reached Helen's shoulder, and she was very slim and sophisticated.

'She reminds me what my name is – when I forget it – and, of course, helps me keep track of just about everything else. She also reminds me that she is French,' added Jack, sotto voce. 'I'm allowed to forget everything but her nationality – which is indelibly stamped on my memory. She appears quite harmless, but let anyone annoy her and *boom!* – there's an explosion. Believe you me, JEACs, you want to be as far away as possible when she's in a temper.'

The children laughed, looking at Monique who just smiled sweetly at Jack without saying a word.

'I don't believe you, Uncle Jack,' said Nimal. 'You must be exaggerating as usual.'

'Moi? Exaggerate? Ask Helen – she, of course, is as mild as a lamb.'

'Are you still here, Jack?' asked Helen amiably, showing the children into a large conference room leading off from her office. 'Both Monique and I do have tempers,' she admitted, 'but we don't often lose them.'

'Quite right, Helen,' agreed Monique from the doorway where she and Jack were standing. 'However, if Jack does not come to his office *immediately* and sign my letters, I will be losing mine shortly.'

'I'm coming,' groaned Jack as he and Monique went off.

Helen invited the children to sit down, gave them something cool to drink, not forgetting Hunter, and then handed out folders.

The covers of the folders had glossy pictures of all kinds of sea creatures, and the smiling faces of dolphins stood out from the rest.

'If you don't mind my calling this important meeting to order,' said Helen with a smile, 'I would like you to open up your folders and take a look at the contents.'

As they complied with her request, she continued, 'There's a detailed and comprehensive map of the site; a list of all the staff and a brief description of the role played by each; pictures and information on all the creatures we hope to have; and of course, lots of fundraising documentation.

'The fundraising material is for a massive mail campaign, and we need to send out approximately 2,000 packages, by the end of this week at the latest. I'm hoping you'll be able to assist us with this mammoth task, starting this afternoon.'

'Sure,' said Anu promptly. 'We often help Mum with mailing campaigns, and have developed a pretty good system.'

'We've done fundraising stuff, too,' said Amy, 'and we'd love to help in any way possible.'

'Good,' said Helen. 'Now, we also need two expert rollerbladers to help with the delivery of documents, and other things, to folks around the site – any takers?' She twinkled at Gina and Mich, who had immediately raised their hands. They were not sure if they could just speak up like the older ones, or if they had to behave as they did in school.

'Well, you two? Game for some hectic rollerblading?' asked Helen genially. 'You don't have to raise your hands, kids, this is all very informal.'

'We can do it,' said Gina brightly. 'Mich and I are very fast on our rollerblades. And Hunter, too – he runs as fast as I can go.'

'I know we'll be able to find everyone, once we study the map a bit,' said Mich hesitantly, 'and it would be great fun, too.'

'Thank you, Mich and Gina,' said Helen warmly. 'A little bird informed me that this job might suit the two of you. Of course, you'll be told exactly where to find the people you are taking a delivery to, and I think it would be good if you went together on deliveries – and Hunter, as well. We'll get knapsacks for the three of you, and a pair of rollerblades for each of you girls – I'm not sure Hunter can rollerblade.'

'We brought our rollerblades with us,' sang out the girls in chorus. 'Our parents said we might be able to use them here.'

'Great! Now, while we're concentrating on the two of you,' continued Helen, ticking off items on the list she had in front of her, 'we need a TV advertisement, geared towards children. It has to be musical and have cartoons, and I understand we have the perfect Larkin and Patel team for such an ad.'

'B-b-but . . .' stammered Gina, 'won't the adults do that? We're just kids.'

'Talented kids, though,' said Helen kindly, smiling at them. 'Yes, normally we would have hired professionals for this task, but Jack had a brainwave. He wanted to involve children in as many aspects of our advertising and shows as possible, and encourage them to participate. That way we appeal even more strongly to children, because they realize that they can be part of this Centre, too. We'd like Rohan and Amy to help you out with ideas of what needs to go into the ad, and to ensure that everything gels. Nimal, if you could help Mich with suggestions about cartoons, that would be perfect. I understand your sketching is excellent.'

'Wow! Sounds fab,' said Amy. 'And what's Anu going to do?'

'Anu will have her hands full – and we've got lots of other tasks for you, too,' said Helen.

'That little bird you mentioned appears to have been quite chatty,' said Rohan with a grin.

Helen nodded as the JEACs laughed, and then continued. 'Now, Nimal – your charisma with animals is well known, and the dolphin playmates – we call them DPs for short – are clamouring to meet you. Now, there's no need to blush like that,' she teased, as Nimal turned red in the face, and the others chuckled. 'They'd like you to work with them, and we wondered if you'd care to be part of their show?'

Nimal was speechless for a few seconds and then gasped, 'Wow – that would be absolutely superfantabulous! When can I start?'

'Soon,' said Helen, 'but what about Hunter? If he's with you, will he be jealous of the dolphins?'

'Oh, no,' said Nimal, 'he's fantastic with all creatures, and never jealous. In fact, he invariably makes friends with any animal that comes to me, and sometimes we see the funniest friendships between them. Plus, he's often with the others, too, and if Gina and Mich are rollerblading all over the place, I'm sure he'll be running with them.'

'Super duper!' said Helen. 'Now, let me tell you what other things we have in store for you. Anu, you may have noticed your name was down on our schedule for a meeting with Jalila?'

Anu nodded.

'Well, we need a writer, and you're the unanimous choice.'

'I told you so,' said Nimal gleefully to Anu, who had turned pale with shock.

Smiling, Helen continued, while Anu listened bemusedly. 'Jalila will meet with you later on this evening and tell you about our thespians – actors,' she explained to Gina and Mich. 'She wants you to come up with your own ideas, so if you could jot down some thoughts prior to meeting her, that would be great. Basically, we need a couple of plays. One for a seal show, involving three adult seals and, if you like, four baby seals. This would be a show for adults and children. Lots of humorous, quick repartee and a simple storyline would be perfect. You and Nimal can work on this together, as he'll be spending a lot of time with the seals, too. We need a second script for an educational piece on conservation, geared for children between the ages of three and six – again, funny and entertaining – in which some of our thespians will participate. If you have the time and energy, we would also like you to write an article on the Conservation, focusing particularly on how teens can get involved. This will be published in the newspapers and some major magazines. Are we asking too much?'

'Well,' said Anu hesitantly, 'it's not too much – but I don't know if my writing's good enough. I've only written plays for small children to act in – not adults. What if . . .'

'Come on, sis,' said Rohan, encouragingly. '*We* know you can do it, and so does Uncle Jack, obviously. Take a shot at it. It's right up your street, and I'm sure there'll be people to help you – won't there, Helen?'

'Of course,' said Helen. 'You can come to Jalila, Monique or myself at any time. Strangely enough, we all majored in English Literature at university; Jalila has studied countless plays, and has a wonderful sense of humour.'

'All right, then – I would love to do it,' said Anu, looking excited.

'Good! Rohan and Amy – we haven't finished with you, yet,' said Helen, perusing her notes once more. 'Rumour has it that the two of you are excellent at waterskiing, right?'

'Er . . . I guess we can both manage it okay,' said Rohan modestly, looking at Amy with a grin.

'I heard otherwise,' said Helen, 'therefore we have a couple of tasks for you. Firstly, sometime this morning, take a good look at the large lake – and meet our four waterskiers, who will be practising, but watching out for you. Observe their skills on waterskis and chat with them – also talk to Jack who can tell you more about their strengths. You will attend the meeting, arranged with them, and we would like you to come up with some snappy dialogue – in simple English, please, as our waterskiers are all Russian and not *totally* comfortable with the language yet. We would also like the two of you to join them in the waterskiing show, while you're with us. Do you mind?'

'Mind?' exclaimed Rohan and Amy, simultaneously.

'No problemo!' said Amy.

'We'll start planning today,' said Rohan.

'Right – that's all for now, folks, and thanks for your co-operation. We'll have lots more for you to do when you're not busy writing, delivering, waterskiing, drawing, et cetera. Do you think we're asking too much?'

'Of course not!' they chorused happily. 'Give us as much as you want.'

'Any questions?' asked Helen, putting her papers together and pouring out more juice for the JEACs.

'Not at the moment – but I'm sure we'll have lots as we go along. Is that okay?' said Anu.

'Sure thing, hon!' said Helen with a smile. 'We'll be meeting like this twice a week, to make sure everything's jogging along smoothly. Also, though I do attend lots of meetings, you can reach me through Joe or Malika, as well as on my mobile, if it's urgent. Right! It's now nearly nine and you need to be at Dolphin Bay by 10:30.'

'What's our programme for the rest of today, Helen?' asked Amy, as everyone gulped down juice.

'If you can bear to tear yourselves away from the site for a while,' smiled Helen, 'we thought that you could go back home at lunchtime, and then start on the mailing – which, as you know, is high priority. All the material is at Jack's place, in the basement office which we use for this sort of work. Do what you can today. Then, take time to think, discuss with each other, and plan the tasks we've set you. Is that all right with you, JEACs?'

'Sure,' said Rohan, the others nodding in agreement. 'We'll do whatever you want us to – even though we're reluctant to leave the site,' he added with a grin.

They all thanked Helen for briefing them.

'Be back here by 12:30, please; I need to give you a sample package of the mail-out. And don't worry about clothes. I'll have some dry things for you to change into before you go home,' said Helen, going to the door with them. 'I hear that you're good timekeepers – see you later!'

She returned to her office, and the JEACs stood outside, gazing around the site and wondering what she meant about dry clothes. But there was no time to worry about that – there was too much to see and do.

They were standing in a pavilion, right in front of the vast, man-made lake. They could see the sky-train tracks and lots of buildings. It was a picturesque setting as the buildings had murals of sea creatures painted on them. Though most of the buildings were ready, there were still dozens of construction workers and staff on the site.

'Wow, what an international team they have,' said Anu, who had buried her nose in the list of staff names. 'We're set for a busy and exciting time, folks! Where should we start, Rohan?'

The others looked at Rohan expectantly, and he said, in a businesslike way, 'Right, let's put our heads together and tell me if you have other ideas, okay?' As the others nodded, he continued, 'It's ten to nine, and we obviously can't see everything today. The Conservation's humongous – but we've lots of time over the next few weeks and, meantime, we have to work on our tasks. So let's begin with the waterskiers, since they'll be watching out for us, and the lake is closest. After them, we'll go straight to Dolphin Bay, because it looks like a good twenty-minute walk to get to it. Right, Anu?'

'Yes,' said Anu, who had her map out. 'We follow this route,' she said, pointing it out to the others. 'Do we go to the bay first or straight to the stands where we can see the dolphins come in?'

'We'd better play that by ear,' said Nimal. 'The DPs will tell us what to do if we get there early.'

'After that,' said Rohan, grinning around at the others, 'I think we'll only have time to get back here for 12:30. Knowing how we're all longing to meet and play with the dolphins, I doubt we'll get away before noon. In fact, I'd better set my watch alarm *now* so that we remember to come back in time. Everyone okay with the plan?'

'Cool,' yelled the JEACs. 'Let's go!'

Ten minutes later, they were chatting with the friendly waterskiers. Rohan and Amy planned to meet with them again soon. Then, waving goodbye, the children set off for Dolphin Bay.

'And now – finally – the dolphins,' said Amy, with a shiver of anticipation.

They passed all kinds of interesting-looking pavilions and enclosures, but could not tell what they were for, as the signs had not been put up yet.

'Look at that mountain,' squealed Mich, pointing to her right. 'There's smoke coming out of the top.'

'It's a man-made mountain, Mich,' said Nimal, who was looking at the map, 'and it's supposed to be volcanic. Watch, it's going to blow its top in a second.'

Sure enough, the mountain rumbled loudly, and smoke, flames and debris shot out of the top. A trough at the foot of the mountain collected the debris which was then channelled back into the mountain. An educational talk about volcanoes would be one of the attractions.

'Gosh, look over there,' said Gina, a few minutes later, as they followed a curve in the pathway. 'A park – full of rides and games. I wish we could go on the rides now,' said the little girl, longingly.

'Me, too,' said Mich, 'but I'm sure we'll get a chance soon.'

'Yeah, after we've finished all our work,' said Gina importantly. 'There's a time and place for everything,' she quoted, in unconscious imitation of her mother.

'You're quite right, Gina,' said Rohan, hiding a grin. 'And you two have an important project to work on.'

'That's true. Oh, what are all these posts with red boxes attached?' asked Mich, pointing to one as they came up to it.

'Probably fire alarms,' said Nimal, examining it. 'Yep – I guess, in case of a fire, they can alert everyone without having to run too far. Cool idea, having them every two hundred metres. I would think each building has one, too – everything here is built with wood.'

'Look, I can see the ocean – we must be close to the bay,' said Rohan.

CHAPTER 10

Amazing Beings

Hastening forward, they reached the entrance to the enclosure, and paused for a moment to drink in the beauty of the scene. It was a natural bay, and the water was light green flecked with white froth as small waves tumbled gently on the sparkling, sandy beach. A large pavilion with murals of dolphins on all the walls was set up near the entrance. The arms of the bay, where the tiered seating and railings were, made an interesting picture and, as Anu said dreamily, 'It looks as if someone is reaching out to give the dolphins a hug and welcome them in.' They all agreed with her.

A large, floating stand was anchored in the middle of the bay and four people waved to them from it. Then, diving into the water, they swam rapidly towards the beach. The children and Hunter scampered down to meet them.

'Hello there,' said the lithe young man who was the first to emerge from the ocean and join them on the little concrete walkway edging the beach. 'I'm Ian, and these are Aneeka, Jane and Chang – and you must be the JEACs! It's great to meet you all. We've heard lots about you!'

The DPs were a joyful and exuberant group, in their mid to late twenties, who were crazy about dolphins and loved to tell stories about them.

'So you're Nimal,' said Ian, smiling at the boy. 'We're eager to see how the dolphins respond to you. It's almost time for them to arrive; we generally meet them at the entrance, and they give us a ride into the bay. We wait for them on the floating stands on either side of the gap – look, you can see them – just outside the bay.'

'And, if you remove your shoes and socks, and come down to the water's edge – it's a good thing you're all wearing shorts – you can play with the dolphins, too,' said Chang. 'Once we stop in the shallow area, we'll call you into the water, and let's see what happens.'

The DPs swam off and clambered up onto the stands.

Removing their footwear hurriedly, the children went down to the water. What would it be like to actually play with dolphins? Did they really like humans, and were they truly as friendly as reported? Well, they would find out soon enough.

'Hunter,' said Nimal to the dog, who was running after the waves, 'sit still now.'

The dog obediently sat down a little distance from the water and watched them curiously.

'What's that funny clicking sound?' asked Gina suddenly. 'And there's a high-pitched whistle, too.'

'It must be the dolphins and their playmates talking to each other,' said Nimal, nearly falling into the sea in his eagerness to get a glimpse of the dolphins.

Moments later they were awestruck when seven huge dolphins came through the gap, leaping in and out of the water, four of them carrying the DPs. Gracefully, playfully and with much clicking and whistling, the dolphin heptad and their playmates came towards the JEACs.

'They *do* have smiley faces,' squealed Gina. 'Oh, they're perfect!'

Each youngster felt a surge of joy as they gazed at the dolphins.

The group came to a halt in the shallows and Aneeka said, 'Space yourselves out – they're big creatures.'

Slowly and quietly the JEACs entered the shallows and waited eagerly to see what would happen next. Nobody said a word.

Then one of the dolphins nosed his way over to where the children were standing. He was simply enormous, and Gina and Mich could not help retreating a little as he swam up. But his gaze was focused on Nimal, who was making small clicking sounds in imitation of those he had heard when the dolphins were entering the bay. As everyone watched breathlessly, the dolphin came right over to Nimal, butted him gently, and then, raising his smiley face, he gave Nimal what sounded like a big, smacking kiss. Seconds later the other dolphins surrounded the boy, all of them trying to touch him. He was ecstatic, though he nearly fell over as the colossal creatures wanted to play with him!

'Wow – you certainly have something special that appeals to them,' said Chang. 'We've never seen them behave like that with anyone else.'

Nimal walked towards the others, the dolphins following him, and soon they had all made friends. The JEACs were thrilled and stroked the dolphins, handing out the fish that the DPs passed on to them. Soon the youngsters were thoroughly soaked, while Gina and Mich had both toppled, head first, into the water, because they could not keep their balance with the dolphins butting into them and wanting to play. They had a phenomenal time!

'What are their names?' asked Nimal, hugging the dolphin who had first come up to him.

'The one you're cuddling,' laughed Jane, 'is Benji. He's the biggest of the heptad, and extremely athletic. He jumps the highest and can turn the most amazing somersaults.

'Over there, with Gina and Mich, are Rosie and Molly. They adore children and are very gentle. I'm sure they would willingly take those two for a ride. Pixie, who is busy communing with Anu, is a little shy, but loves being stroked, and will do anything for her favourite fish!'

'That's Gip, with Rohan,' continued Aneeka, 'Pixie's mate. He's another athlete, though not as big and strong as Benji. And Vol, who's butting Amy, is Molly's mate and extremely powerful. He's bigger than Benji, though not as athletic. But he can carry all four of us on his back with ease, and probably more, if necessary.'

'Where's the last one?' asked Nimal, looking around.

The next minute he was flying through the air on the back of the seventh dolphin, who had dived between his legs underwater. With a wide grin on its smiley face, it took Nimal for a ride in the shallows. Nimal was plonked back in the water, drenched to the skin, but laughing delightedly – the dolphin butting him, playfully, and giving him loud, smacking kisses.

Everyone roared with laughter and the dolphin raised himself upright and did a sort of shimmy, which made it appear as though he were laughing, too.

'And that,' said Aneeka, when she had stopped laughing, 'is Billy – our comedian! He's totally incorrigible and you never know what he'll be up to next. You can see he enjoys making us laugh!'

'Let's get Hunter now, and watch the fun,' said Nimal, after he had given Billy lots of hugs. 'Hunter – here, boy!'

The dog trotted over to the water's edge obediently, and everyone watched to see what would happen.

Nimal encouraged Hunter into the sea, and Billy immediately came up to check out what was going on. Nimal spoke softly to Hunter, 'It's okay, boy, it's a friend. His name is Billy.'

Billy and Hunter looked at each other. Hunter sat down in the water and waved a paw in the air – his mouth opened in a friendly grin as he made soft whining noises to the dolphin. Billy looked at the friendly dog, and then gently took Hunter's paw in his large mouth and shook it, clicking rapidly as he did so. It was quite incredible, and the humans could scarcely believe their eyes.

'I wonder if they have a medium they can communicate in,' said Ian thoughtfully, gazing at the two creatures.

'Gee, just look at them now,' exclaimed Amy, as Billy and Hunter began a game of what looked like 'catch me if you can' along the water's edge – the dog darting into the water, the dolphin backing off and then chasing Hunter back to the beach. 'One would think they'd grown up together!'

The other dolphins wanted to make friends with Hunter, too, but the sight of seven enormous creatures all coming towards him at once was a bit too much for Hunter. He backed out of the water rapidly, and sat on the beach, waving one paw in the air and barking at them. Billy, appearing to understand Hunter's reluctance to play with the heptad, chased the others away and then went back to where Hunter was, making loud kissing noises this time and trying to persuade his friend to come back and play.

Time flew by and, all too soon, the dolphins swam away.

As the group dripped up the beach to sit in the pavilion, the talk turned to how Nimal could participate in the show, and they agreed to meet later and discuss this in detail.

'Can't we join in, too?' begged Gina and Mich.

'Actually, I was just thinking of that,' said Chang. 'It would be great for the spectators to see a couple of small kids – no offence, girls – playing with the dolphins, and Hunter as well. Are the two of you good swimmers?'

'Like fish,' said Nimal immediately, 'and that's a fab idea. There would be a heptad of humans, too. Do you think anyone will mind?'

'No,' said Ian. 'The only concern would be if they were not great in the water, or if Jack felt it was dangerous, but we could keep them in the bay area. Let's work on it.'

They agreed enthusiastically. Clearly, the JEACs had fallen in love with the dolphins. As for Nimal, he was in a daze. Anu and Rohan looked at him closely, winked at each other and left him alone.

The DPs gave the children towels so that they could dry off a little bit.

'*Now* I understand what Helen meant when she said she would have some other clothes for us,' said Rohan, giving up his attempt to squeeze water out of his heavy denim shorts. 'We sure could use some dry clothes. But it was definitely worth getting wet, and next time we'll bring our swimsuits.'

'You folk are so lucky,' said Amy to the DPs. 'I hope you're still here when I've finished my training and come back to work with Uncle Jack.'

Just then Rohan's alarm went off. After thanking the DPs profusely, they started back to meet Helen at the office.

'Is Nimal okay?' whispered Amy to Anu as they followed the boys. 'He's been rather quiet – unusual for him.'

'He's fine,' said Anu softly. 'But don't be surprised if he joins you in working for Uncle Jack. He'll be okay once he's had a chat with Rohan.'

'He and you are very close, aren't you?' said Amy, looking at the pretty girl, curiously.

'Oh, we're all very close,' said Anu. 'After all, we grew up together.'

'You're sure lucky to have two wonderful brothers,' said Amy enviously.

'Well, Gina and I think we are,' said Anu, 'but we don't tell the boys in case they get swollen heads! You're welcome to share them, and Hunter, too – in any case, I feel as if we're all one big family.' She linked her arm affectionately in Amy's.

'I feel the same, Anu,' said Amy, squeezing her arm. 'You're a great sister to have, and Gina's a pet!'

Rohan and Nimal were having a fairly serious conversation.

'You'll probably think I'm crazy,' said Nimal, 'but I *definitely* want to work with dolphins. They're extraordinary beings and I want to know as much about them as possible. I'm still going to be a conservationist and a naturalist, but I'll specialize with dolphins. Do you think I'm nuts, or being too impulsive again?'

'No, yaar – not this time,' said Rohan. 'I think you've found your true love where conservation is concerned, and I can't imagine a more amazing group of creatures to work and play with. Good for you – now you have a focus. Let's chat tonight in our room, and if Uncle Jack's free, perhaps he'd come up and join us.'

'Thanks, yaar,' said Nimal gratefully. 'Will you ask him? I feel a bit awkward, surprisingly.'

'No problemo,' said Rohan. 'Here we are – boy, the walk back didn't take much time at all.'

'Helen! Helen!' shrieked Mich and Gina, running up to her, their faces glowing with joy. 'We played with the dolphins – they're fantastic – they all loved Nimal – Hunter also played with them . . .'

'I'm so glad – although it's what we expected. And the lot of you are soaking wet – also as expected!' said Helen with a laugh, fending off the two little girls who were dancing around her. 'I love the dolphins dearly, but I have an external meeting to attend and you smell distinctly fishy at the moment. In that building next door, you'll find ladies' and gents' showers, changing rooms and fresh, dry clothes laid out.'

She shooed them off, adding, 'Join me in my office when you're ready and leave the wet clothes in the changing rooms. Oh, and give Hunter a shower in there, too.'

It did not take them long to shower and change and soon all of them were ready. They bounced back into Helen's office, chattering nineteen to the dozen, telling Helen, Joe and Malika all about the dolphins.

The adults listened in amusement, wishing they, too, could have seen the dolphins surrounding Nimal and playing with Hunter. Then Helen took the children into the conference room again, and gave them something to drink, as they were very thirsty.

'How tired are you?' she asked.

'Not a bit,' said Nimal promptly. 'In fact, I feel as if I've been given an extra dose of energy.'

For once no one laughed at him or teased him about having an excess of energy. Helen smiled understandingly.

'Time with the dolphins tends to affect most people that way,' she said, 'which is why we're so keen on encouraging people to learn about them.'

The JEACs nodded in agreement, and Amy added, 'I also feel as if I don't need to worry about anything ever again.'

'That's another reaction many of us have, and I'm glad you children had this stimulating experience. It will, I believe, make you even more enthusiastic – if that's possible – about helping with all the mundane tasks this afternoon, like mailings.'

'That's not mundane at all,' said Anu. 'In fact, it's a lot of fun.'

Helen handed the sample package to Anu. Giving them a few more instructions, she took them out to the parking lot, where they thanked her for everything.

'I should be the one thanking you,' said Helen beaming at them and bending down to pat Hunter. 'It's been delightful meeting all of you, and I'm looking forward to having you here on site. Now, if you have any questions about the mailing, don't hesitate to call me, okay?'

'Sure,' said Anu.

Just then Mike arrived and, waving goodbye to Helen, they set off for home. Mike agreed to hear about the dolphins at the same time as Aunty Meg and Jack, so during the drive back home, they talked instead about their conversation with the waterskiers and what Helen had asked each of them to do.

Over a nice hot lunch, they told Jack, Mike and Aunty Meg about their time with the dolphins, amusing them with Hunter and Billy's antics, and how the dolphins had loved Nimal. Listening to them and watching their glowing faces, Jack knew he had made the right decision in inviting them over to be involved in the opening of the Conservation.

CHAPTER 11

Fundraising Mail-outs and Brainstorming

'So, what's the programme for this afternoon and evening?' asked Aunty Meg, as the children paused in their chatter to finish off with dessert.

'We're going to deal with the mailing,' said Rohan, 'and if I know Anu, she'll keep our noses to the grindstone until we've finished.'

'Whoa!' exclaimed Jack, 'I thought there were around 2,000 people receiving this mailing. You can't possibly do it all today – even though you are a sensational group! I'm sure Helen didn't expect you to complete the job in one afternoon.'

'It's not such a big deal, Uncle Jack,' said Anu, grinning at him. 'There are seven of us and, if you come down a bit later, you'll see what I mean by teamwork. The four of us have handled larger mail-outs than this, for Mum and Aunty Nancy.' She laughed as she saw the astonished looks on the adults' faces, and continued, 'I promise you – I'm not exaggerating! Just wait and see. Mike, do you remember our mail-outs?'

'Sure do – and she's right, Jack,' said Mike. 'She's a great organizer and they're a good team.'

The JEACs rose from the table, eager to start their task.

'What about tea? And would you like some juice downstairs?' asked Aunty Meg.

Everyone looked at Anu.

'It's 1:15 now,' said Anu, glancing at her watch. 'Could we have tea around 4:30, Aunty Meg? We'll come up for it, though, and take a fifteen-minute break – and we'd love some juice downstairs, if it's not too much trouble.'

'Certainly, love,' said Aunty Meg.

Ten short minutes later, under Anu's directions, everything was set up – including the postage meter and boxes into which the completed packages would be placed, ready for Mike and the boys to take to the post office later on in the evening.

'We're going to finish this task by 7 p.m. at the latest,' said Anu with determination. 'Excluding our fifteen-minute tea break, that gives us approximately five hours and fifteen minutes of solid work.'

'Slave driver,' muttered Nimal, pretending to glower at her. He was back to his teasing self again. 'Pax! I will be good, Aunty,' he moaned, as Anu grabbed him by the ear and led him to his place.

Laughing, they settled down to work, and an hour later, when the three adults came down to see how they were doing, they could not believe their eyes at the rapid, methodical and efficient way in which the work was being done.

'Incredible,' said Jack, 'even Hunter has a task. Now, let's see if I can figure out what each of you is doing. Is this a general mailing or a personalized one?'

'General, Uncle Jack,' said Anu. 'We'd have to work differently if it was a personalized one, and it would take much longer.'

Jack nodded and continued, 'So, Anu folds the letters, Rohan collates the four pamphlets, Nimal takes a letter and a set of pamphlets and stuffs them in an envelope which he piles up in front of Amy. Amy sticks on a label and passes it to Mich, who seals it and places it in front of Gina. Gina runs it through the postage meter and drops it in the box, ready for mailing. Hunter wanders around, supervising, encouraging and giving general advice, and also picking up the occasional envelope that falls outside the box and putting it back in. What a fantastic team!'

Showering them with praise, the adults left them to their task, Jack and Mike returning to the Conservation, while Aunty Meg busied herself around the house.

The children enjoyed their work immensely. It was great to be together, their tongues wagging incessantly while their hands were busy. At 4:30 sharp, Anu called a halt – she had asked Rohan to set the alarm on his watch – and they trooped upstairs for tea.

'How is it going?' asked Aunty Meg. 'Helen called but I told her you were too busy to talk to her then, so perhaps you could call her, Anu.'

'Sure,' said Anu. 'I think she'll be surprised to hear that we'll be finished by seven. May I use the phone here, Aunty Meg?'

Aunty Meg nodded, and Anu called Helen and updated her. Helen was not just surprised, she was flabbergasted!

'What do you mean, by seven?' she demanded. 'You surely don't mean tonight? Jack and Mike told us that you were going great guns, but I didn't expect this!'

'We're having a blast,' said Anu, 'and if you have any more mailings you need help with while we're here, we'd be happy to do them.'

'Amazing! Unbelievable! Awesome!' muttered Helen over the telephone. 'I can see I'll have my hands full trying to keep you lot occupied.'

'Don't worry,' chuckled Anu, 'we can also amuse ourselves. I have to run now, Helen,' she continued, 'our break's nearly up.'

'Thanks very much,' said Helen, 'and please thank the others for me, too. Don't kill yourselves over this task though, right?'

'We won't – bye for now,' said Anu, and rang off.

She told the others about Helen's reaction and how delighted she was that they would complete the job the same day. Everyone was glad, because they had taken an instinctive liking to the jovial woman, and they were happy to be part of the team.

By seven they were done, and the boys carried the heavy boxes up the stairs. They had just piled them neatly on the porch when Mike arrived in the Land Rover.

'I'm seeing visions,' he muttered, blinking in amazement. 'Well, you folks have done a super job. Let's get these into the Land Rover – does anyone want to come for a ride?'

They all went, except for Anu, who said she wanted to think about her writing and sketch out some ideas. While they were gone, she drafted the outline for the children's piece. She also put down points to discuss with Jalila about the adult play, and made notes on what she thought could be included in the article; after this she joined Aunty Meg on the front lawn.

'What are you going to do till dinner time?' asked Aunty Meg as the others joined her and Anu.

Mike had gone back to supervise the setting up of the stage for the campaign, which was to be held in a large park so that passers-by would be attracted to it.

'Can Mich and I rollerblade, Aunty Meg?' begged Gina. 'We could practise for our courier job.'

'Sure, honey,' said Aunty Meg, with a smile. 'Just don't go near the river, all right?'

'We won't, Aunty,' said Mich. 'Hunter can run with us.'

They ran off to get their rollerblades.

'I need to think about the panel discussion tomorrow,' said Rohan, 'and if you three are free, a brainstorming session would be good – it'll help all of us in our various tasks.'

'Yes, I need material for the article, and Nimal and I could use some suggestions for the seal show,' said Anu.

'Yeah, and we can come up with ideas for the kiddies' ad,' said Amy. 'When do you think we should talk to them about it?'

'Tomorrow morning would do,' said Rohan. 'I checked with Mike about tomorrow, and he said it would be best if we worked on our tasks at home. They're trying to complete all the major construction at the site over the next couple of days, and there will be around 400 extra people working there.'

'Whew, that'll cost a mint,' said Nimal, with a whistle.

'All 400 are volunteer construction workers,' said Rohan, 'and each of them has given up a vacation day to work on the site. Amazing, isn't it? It'll be featured on TV so we'll see them on the late night news, probably with a bit about the campaign thrown in.'

'What time does the campaign start?' asked Amy.

'5:30 – for two hours,' said Rohan.

Anu got up and stretched out a hand to assist Aunty Meg to her feet. 'Do you need us to do anything for you before we start our brainstorming session, Aunty?'

'Nothing, thank you, dear,' said Aunty Meg. 'Do you think you'll survive till dinner time – 9:30 tonight if you want to wait for Mike and Jack – or would you like a snack now?'

'A tiny nibble would be perfect, Aunty, dear,' said Nimal, falling over Hunter who bounced up at him exuberantly.

Aunty Meg chuckled, smiling at him as he lay on the ground, Hunter on top of him. 'You are quite incorrigible, Nimal,' she said. 'Are you always so klutzy?'

'You cut me to the quick, Aunty Meg,' said Nimal, with a woebegone look. 'I'm as dainty as any fairy – most of the time. It's this wretched dog – he trips me up on purpose!'

'Fairy! Huh! Dainty as an ephalunt, more like,' said Rohan. He ducked Nimal's quick karate chop and ran into the house, calling to the girls, 'Meet you in the library.'

Chuckling, they went back to the house, leaving Hunter to race with the little girls. Aunty Meg promised to send a snack to the library and arrange one for the girls and Hunter, too.

Armed with notebooks and pencils, the four older ones settled down to a serious brainstorming session and came up with loads of ideas and suggestions.

Then they split up, Rohan and Amy discussing the waterskiing, while Anu and Nimal planned the seal show. At dinner time they stopped, satisfied with what they had accomplished.

'Tomorrow we'll work individually or in teams,' said Rohan, as they moved towards the dining room. 'You've got the most difficult task,

Anu – and I know you need peace and quiet to write. So why don't you choose your spot first.'

'Could I use the library?' asked Anu. 'Then, if I need to look up anything, it's right there. Plus,' she added with a grin, 'I always write better when I'm surrounded by books.'

'Deal,' said Rohan, giving her a quick hug. 'But beware, sis – you'll turn into a little green bookworm one of these days.'

They entered the dining room to find the others already there, including Jalila, Czainski and Padmini.

'Where's Okanu?' asked Nimal, taking his place at the table.

'He's spending the night on site as he's very busy and will be up extremely early in the morning, but you'll see him at the campaign,' said Jack. 'So, what did you folk do this evening? Our two little couriers look quite exhausted and I think it's an early night for them – what do you say, children?'

'I don't mind,' said Mich promptly, and Gina nodded in agreement. They both looked rather drowsy.

After the meal the two little girls said goodnight and trundled off to bed. Jalila and Anu spent fifteen minutes together.

'Just go right ahead, Anu,' said Jalila enthusiastically, after listening to Anu's ideas. 'We're on the same wavelength, and I like your plans very much indeed. Have confidence in yourself, my dear,' she continued kindly, as Anu looked a bit hesitant. 'Do you think you could have a first draft of the educational piece by tomorrow, or is that asking too much?'

'No problemo,' said Anu eagerly. 'You'll have it by lunchtime.'

Meanwhile, Rohan and Jack were in the study, on a conference call with Helen. They talked about the panel discussion for the next day, and agreed with Helen's suggestion that Jack field all questions and direct them to whichever panel member was best suited to respond. Rohan felt more relaxed after the call. Just before they left the study, he asked Jack if he could spare them half an hour before they went to bed – explaining that Nimal needed some career counselling. Jack was happy to oblige, and they returned to the living room where the others were chatting desultorily.

'Looks like bedtime for most of us,' said Jack with a grin. 'Even Hunter's yawning. Off you go youngsters – thanks for all your help, and have a good sleep.'

Yawning and bidding everyone goodnight, they went upstairs. The girls fell asleep quickly, Anu setting her alarm for 4 a.m. as she was eager to get started on her writing.

The boys had a helpful talk with Jack and then went to bed. Nimal, feeling very positive about his new focus, dreamed of dolphins and Hunter all night long.

CHAPTER 12

Hard Work and the Awareness Campaign

Tuesday dawned and Anu woke up before her alarm went off. Without disturbing Gina, she had a quick shower, dressed, and went downstairs. Aunty Meg always made sure there was coffee, tea, juice and biscuits available in the dining room for early risers, and Anu helped herself to some of it and went into the library.

She settled down and started her piece for the three to six-year-olds. By the time the others called her for breakfast at 8 a.m., she had completed a first draft.

After a quick meal, Anu sent the draft to Jalila, via Joe, who came by to pick up something from the house. She then returned to the library while Rohan, Amy and Nimal sat down with the younger girls, and gave them some ideas for the cartoon advertisement. Gina and Mich were eager to get started, so after the session with the three older ones, they went off to discuss it on their own, feeling very important indeed. Nimal left Rohan and Amy to talk about their waterskiing and joined Anu in the library to toss around ideas about the play involving the seals.

Other than a short break for lunch, they all worked hard and the day sped by. By 3 p.m. each of them had a pretty good picture of what they had to do. The older ones were ready with drafts and plans of how they would accomplish their tasks. Gina was in her room working on the wording of the song for the advertisement. Mich, with Nimal's help, was drawing cartoons of various sea creatures.

'Gee, the day sure disappeared, didn't it?' said Amy in surprise, when Nimal poked his head into the living room to say that it was time to get ready for the campaign.

'Sure did,' said Rohan. 'This is cool! I wish we had more projects at school. How are Mich and Gina doing, Nimal?'

'Great,' said Nimal. 'Gina's finished the song and says she'll polish it after the campaign. Then Mich will work on the cartoons and they should be ready by Wednesday, lunchtime.'

'By the way,' he continued, 'I spoke to Uncle Jack just now, and he said that since we'll be living on site from tomorrow evening onwards, we should finalize everything here in the morning, and go to the Centre around 4 p.m. I told him we'd do whatever he thought was best. Right?'

'Right on, boy,' said Anu joining them. 'I've finished the writing, Nimal. If you and I do a conference call with Jalila and the actors tonight, after the campaign, we can finalize both plays.'

'Brainwave, sis,' said Rohan, 'and Amy and I can do one with the waterskiers, too, with help from Uncle Jack as interpreter, if necessary.'

'Good,' said Nimal, 'so we'll all be ready with our tasks. Hopefully, they won't need too much revision.'

'Okay – then we'd better get ready for this evening. Hope it goes smoothly,' said Rohan.

They ran upstairs and found Mich and Gina chatting in one of the bedrooms.

By 4:45 they were ready, and Hunter was left behind to keep Aunty Meg company, as there would be a large crowd at the campaign.

It only took them ten minutes to reach the park where the campaign was to take place. An enormous stage had been set up, with an excellent public address system so that everyone could hear clearly, and people were already gathering round. The JEACs met up with other staff from the Centre – all those who could leave the site were there – and sat down amidst them. Rohan, Mike and Jack went behind the stage and joined Helen. They were early – Ingram and his team were nowhere to be seen. A few minutes later, Judge Dickinson arrived, and Rohan was introduced to him.

'I am pleased to see young folk participating in these discussions, Rohan,' said Judge Dickinson. 'Welcome to Australia! I'll see you at the fundraising event on the twenty-second, too.'

He moved away to chat with Jack and Mike; Rohan, who was beginning to feel a little nervous, hung out with Helen. However, her cheerful talk and sense of humour soon calmed him down and he peered out from behind the stage at the park, which was almost full, despite its size. The 1,000 seats set up for the event were already occupied, and people were now sitting on the grass, park benches and lawn chairs, or just milling about. Mounted police and other officers were also present, as was a large TV crew.

It was nearly time for the event to start – the panel discussion was not scheduled till 6:15 and would end the campaign.

'I guess Ingram feels that he doesn't need to show up till he takes the stage,' whispered Helen to Rohan, as the curtains rose and Jack went on stage to welcome the crowd and thank them for attending.

'Friends,' said Jack, 'here's a quick outline of our programme. We'll commence with music from the well-known band *Energy Conservation*, who will sing some of their popular numbers. Next, there will be a short slide show about our new Centre and its special features; and then fifteen minutes during which you can ask questions of my colleague, Mike Carpenter, and myself. This will be followed by a short play performed by teenagers from the *Young Conservationists'* group in Melbourne. They are visiting the Gold Coast and have been kind enough to join us this evening – the play is about the dangers of deforestation and the effects on our world. Finally, there will be a panel discussion with Judge Dickinson as the moderator. I hope you enjoy the evening, and thank you, once again, for your presence and support.'

Jack walked off the stage to the sound of loud cheering and clapping. He was a popular figure in the community.

The crowd responded positively to the programme, which incorporated a great deal of humour, despite the serious nature of the subject. However, one bunch of teenagers appeared to be begging for trouble. At every opportunity, they booed and jeered, especially when the Melbourne group came on, and the police had a busy time controlling the troublemakers and preventing them from throwing fruit and vegetables at the group. These malcontents were standing fairly close to the stage.

Czainski, who was nearby, muttered, 'Look over there, Okanu, to your left – that chap in the bright blue T-shirt – isn't he Darrel Owen's son, George?'

'Sure looks like it,' said Okanu, 'and he appears to be the chief instigator of the trouble caused by that group of kids. I think I'll move over to stand next to that policeman – right behind George – coming?'

'Lead on,' said Czainski grimly. 'We might as well be there if they get out of hand.'

With some difficulty they moved into position. When they saw Okanu's bulk right behind them, the teens tried to edge away, but the packed crowd prevented them from doing so and they were compelled to remain where they were.

Meanwhile, backstage, Rohan and the others were getting ready to go on for the panel discussion, scheduled to start in five minutes, and there was still no sign of Ingram. However, two minutes before they were due on stage, Ingram walked up, with Darrel beside him – Rohan recognized them immediately. Right behind them were another man and a teenager.

Rohan's fists clenched; it was Don, the boy who had accosted Amy at the Big Pineapple and spat at Nimal and him.

'Helen,' whispered Rohan, 'is that Mr. Ingram's son?'

'Yeah,' said Helen. 'Do you know him? He's a nasty piece of work.'

'We've met!' said Rohan grimly. 'Tell you later.'

Jack was welcoming the other team. Rohan knew that Don recognized him, too, and though neither boy made any mention of their meeting, Don made an obscene gesture when the adults weren't looking. Rohan stared back at him scornfully.

Once on stage, Judge Dickinson introduced the members of each team. The fourth member of Ingram's team was Eugene, a staff member from the lodge. Then Jack asked if someone from the audience would like to join the pro-conservation team. A young woman was quick to raise her hand and was warmly welcomed; she took her place next to Helen.

Judge Dickinson informed the audience that he had drawn up some frequently asked questions for both teams, and that there would be a period for audience participation during which time any questions could be raised.

It was a sizzling session! Ingram had obviously rounded up a group of supporters who booed Jack's team and vociferously cheered his own. Ingram thumped the table, accused Jack of trying to harm his business, and made all manner of nasty insinuations about Jack's motives for starting a conservation in the Gold Coast. When it was Don's turn to speak, he was very aggressive and showed his contempt for conservationists by running down their ideas. He was encouraged by the teenagers who, led by his friend George, cheered him on loudly. Rohan was calm – his lucidity and obvious love for conservation, and animals in particular, earned him a thundering applause.

This proved too much for Don who, glaring at Rohan, growled into the microphone (which his anger had unfortunately made him forget was in front of him), 'You think you're so great – moron! Why don't you just go home and stop trying to tell us how to do things here, you . . . you . . . ignoramus!'

There was dead silence for a moment as Don's statement came loud and clear over the PA system. Rohan turned pale with anger, but Jack laid a hand on his shoulder and he managed to control his temper. Then boos and hisses broke out from the crowd as they yelled at Don to apologize.

Judge Dickinson, looking disgusted, turned to Don and John Ingram, expecting them to apologize, but while Ingram signalled his son to hold his tongue, neither of them spoke.

Judge Dickinson rose from his seat and said, 'All right, everybody, please calm down. *Calm down*! I think we will draw this discussion to a close. Before we do so, however, I would like to remind you that what we have heard tonight gives us a picture of what our world is facing. We need to reflect on it and decide, for ourselves, what stand we will take. I thank you for your patience during this discussion. Goodnight.'

He sat down, and Jack thanked the crowd and brought the campaign to a close.

Ingram, Don and Eugene left the stage hurriedly, not even stopping to thank Judge Dickinson or Jack. Darrel Owen hung back, for a few minutes, to thank Jack perfunctorily for letting them participate and to half-apologize for Don's rudeness, attempting to laugh it off by saying 'Well, you know – boys are always so competitive.' His statement was received in a stony silence, then Jack and Mike said goodnight and moved away to speak to other people.

Rohan and Helen were boiling with anger. As they waited for the others to join them, Rohan told her about their first encounter with Don.

'But we didn't know he was Mr. Ingram's son,' he concluded. 'Oh, man, Amy looks madder than a wet hen,' he added as the others joined them.

'That idiot! That absolute piece of garbage,' burst out Amy, explosively. 'Where does he think he gets off behaving like that? And his father – he didn't say one word in apology. You should have said something, Rohan.'

'And lower himself to Don's standards? I think not,' said Jack coming up with Mike. 'I'm really sorry, son,' he said putting an arm around Rohan's shoulders, 'and I apologize for exposing you to Don in front of the crowds. But I must confess, I never expected him to behave like that in public. I'm impressed with your self-control.'

Rohan was too angry to reply. Nimal, like Amy, was fuming – but knowing Rohan was frothing mad and needed time to work off his anger, he didn't say anything either.

They piled into the vehicle and were soon back home.

What a tirade of anger broke out the minute they entered the living room. Every one of the children – excepting Rohan – had something to say, and Jack listened to them all, wisely letting them vent their feelings.

After they had talked themselves out, Jack said, 'Rohan, you haven't said anything so far – it's your turn.'

'Uncle Jack,' growled Rohan, struggling to control his temper, 'I'm so angry I don't know what to say! I wish . . .' He trailed off, punched his fist into the air, and continued with a wry grin, 'I'm trying to console myself with the fact that most of the crowd was obviously on my side. I think I'll go to your gym and use your punching bag – I'll pretend it's Don's head.'

'Go ahead, my boy,' said Jack understandingly. 'See you in a bit.'

Rohan raised his eyebrows at Nimal, who promptly joined him, and the two of them went down to the gym. They had a strenuous workout, Rohan pummelling the punching bag furiously. Then, after a quick shower, they joined the others for dinner.

Everyone was more relaxed by then, and they discussed the rest of the campaign over dinner. After a talk with Rohan and Nimal, which made both boys feel comfortable once more, Jack left to do some work in his office. Gina and Mich went off together, Gina to finalize her song, and Mich to do some more sketches, while the four older ones gathered in the library.

By mutual agreement, none of them discussed the campaign, but concentrated on the tasks they had to complete by the next day. It had been an exhausting day, though, and they did not stay up too long. By 9:30 all of them were fast asleep.

CHAPTER 13

The Fruits of Labour

After breakfast, the JEACs rushed upstairs to pack their knapsacks. They were very excited about spending the next few weeks on site, and Mike had already dropped off their suitcases at the Conservation.

'What time is Helen arriving, Anu?' asked Gina.

'Two o'clock,' said Anu, 'and then we'll have our meeting so she can see what we've done so far. How are you and Mich doing with the ad?'

'It's finished,' said Gina. 'Mich has done the cartoons, Nimal and Rohan will scan them into the computer this morning, and then we'll sing it at the meeting while the computer projects the cartoons onto a screen.'

'Fantastic! What a super idea to scan them and do a complete presentation – very professional indeed,' said Anu, hugging the little girl. 'Mum and Dad will be so proud, and I'm longing to hear it.'

'It was Nimal's idea to scan the cartoons,' said Gina.

'Cool,' said Anu, as they ran downstairs to join the others.

'Aunty Meg,' said Mich, 'you will come to our meeting with Helen, won't you?'

'Yes, of course, dear,' said Aunty Meg, smiling at the eager little girl. 'I hear that you and Gina are going to sing us your advertisement – and I wouldn't miss that for the world. Actually, Jack just called and said that the entire Management Team would be here, as they wanted to hear everything.'

'Awesome!' chorused Gina and Mich.

'Now we have to do the scanning,' said Mich importantly. 'Nimal and Rohan, could you please come with us?'

'Of course, your majesties,' said Nimal, bowing deeply and gesturing for the girls to go through the door first. 'Anything your highnesses say!'

The others went over their tasks, too, putting finishing touches to them and hoping that the Management Team would approve.

'Lunchtime,' called Aunty Meg at 1 p.m. The children ran to the dining room and found the adults already seated.

'I'm starving,' said Nimal pathetically. 'You can't imagine what a rough time I had trying to keep up with two incorrigible juvenile delinquents. They kept our noses to the grindstone!'

'Good for them,' said Jack, smiling at the excited girls. 'And are you all ready for the meeting? I'm eager to see what you've come up with.'

'Hope they'll be okay,' said Anu a little nervously. 'We've done the best we can.'

'Then it's sure to be good,' said Jack with a smile of encouragement. 'Let's eat quickly and then move into the living room.'

Lunch had never been gobbled down so fast. By 1:30 the youngsters were finished and asked to be excused so that they could set up everything in the living room.

The adults joined them at two, and once everyone was settled comfortably, the ideas were presented.

Rohan and Amy went first. They said their basic plan was to involve the spectators in the waterskiing show by dividing them into two groups, one for each team of waterskiers. There would be no serious competition as such, but they would get the two groups to cheer as loudly as possible and give points to the teams based on the cheers. Rohan divided the people in the room and he and Amy demonstrated their idea. They had also drawn up a tentative programme for the show.

'Great job, you two,' said Helen enthusiastically, as everyone clapped at the end of their presentation. 'I think it'll work well and, don't forget, as you work with the team, you may find that you want to add or change certain things – and that's fine with us. What do the rest of you think?' she concluded, turning to the other adults.

'Fantastic,' said Jack immediately, and the others nodded in agreement.

They made a few suggestions which were gratefully accepted.

Rohan and Amy relaxed, pleased that their work was acceptable.

Anu and Nimal then spoke briefly about the seal show.

'We've decided to use all three adult seals, the four seal pups, three actors, Nimal and Hunter,' began Anu.

'Nimal will be the teacher at a school attended by the four pups and Hunter. There'll be all kinds of funny things that happen in the school.

Then, one day, two rogues – a seal and one of the actors – come along and steal a pup. They run away and hide in an underwater cave, forgetting that the human can't breathe underwater. So the human keeps popping up for air; his friend, the seal, gets very annoyed with him and they have a fight.'

'Then a chief constable comes along with three policemen,' continued Nimal, 'which are, of course, two actors and two seals, and they start searching for the bad guys. The remaining seal pups, the dog and their teacher decide to follow and help the policemen and, naturally, there's a lot of confusion. The pups get in everyone's way, Hunter bites the wrong people, while, in the background, the bad guy and the seal are popping up for air but nobody notices them.'

'Finally, the culprits are caught and the pup rescued,' concluded Anu. 'The rogues promise never to do anything like that again; as punishment, they are sent to school for a month and have to join the pups in learning how to count, and sing "Ring around the Roses".'

'And here's a bit of the dialogue,' said Nimal, handing out scripts to Rohan and Amy.

The four of them acted out a small part of a scene, Hunter joining in, and the whole room roared with laughter at the comic lines. Jalila, in particular, was thrilled, and begged to be the 'bad guy'.

'Superb job, Anu,' said Helen, wiping tears of mirth from her eyes.

'Nimal helped a lot,' said Anu. 'I got most of the laughter lines from him.'

After a few suggestions from the Management Team, Anu spoke briefly about her educational piece for the little children.

Six adults would dress up as sea creatures – dolphin, shark, turtle, seal, seahorse and blue whale, and pretend they lived in tanks. They would tell the children about themselves. Simple, comic lines would be used. At the end of the show, the baby seals would be brought in and the children would be allowed to stroke them, if they wished.

Jalila, who had already seen the script, told the others that it was extremely well written, would take about twenty minutes, and would work very well. She had already chosen the actors for the show.

The Management Team was delighted with Anu's ideas.

Finally, Nimal and Rohan turned on the computer and projector. Mich and Gina, looking rather nervous but determined, stood together on one side of the screen and Nimal explained what they were going to do.

'We've scanned the cartoons into the computer and as Mich and Gina sing, I'll run the cartoons on the screen.'

'Very impressive,' said Jack.

'Ready, girls?' asked Nimal, and as they nodded, he started the show.

A beautiful sketch of the Conservation, with its name, came up first – this was the only slide drawn by Nimal. The next slide had a title which read 'JOIN US, PLEASE!' with cartoons of smiling dolphins and other sea creatures beckoning the onlookers. Then the two girls began to sing to a tune similar to that of 'Oh my darling, Clementine', Gina singing the main tune, and Mich harmonizing.

> In the Gold Coast of Australia
> There's a place you want to be
> It is called a con-ser-vation
> And has creatures from the sea!
>
> Sharks and whales and seals and turtles,
> And of course there's Dolphin Bay,
> Where the dolphins come and greet you
> And with them you'll want to play!
>
> Come and see them, they're fantastic
> And there's tons of things to do,
> Rides and fun shows, education,
> Lots of eating places, too.
>
> Twenty-second of December
> Aquatic Fantasia and Dolphin Bay
> Welcomes all you special people
> To our fun-filled Opening Day.
>
> Come and join us, learn about them
> Understand our passion, too.
> Con-ser-vation is important
> Saves the world for me and you!

As they sang, the cartoons changed, beautifully drawn and coloured. All of them were funny and matched the words of the song – the timing was perfect.

There was a dead silence as the girls finished and the screen went blank. Then the room resounded with cheers, catcalls, whistles and clapping. Jack rose and went over to pick up both girls in a bear hug, and everyone commented on the excellent job they had done.

'We had lots of help from the others,' said Gina modestly.

But everyone in the room knew that she had a true gift, while Mich was an extraordinarily talented cartoonist.

'Thank you all; it's unbelievable,' said Helen. 'You know, when I was told that each of you JEACs had special talents, and then I met you, I knew you would do a good job. However, I did not expect everything to be so professional and thorough. You're superb and, believe me, we're extremely grateful. Thank you very much indeed.'

Jack and Mike were beaming around, with 'I told you so' faces, when Jalila said, 'Do you think we could ask you to go one step further?'

'Sure,' said Rohan, and the others nodded eagerly.

'Well, I think it would be even better if all of you sang the ad rather than us getting a professional group to do it. We could arrange for you to practise with a band, and at the end of the ad we could flash a picture of all of you. What do you think, Czainski? Don't you think that would have a stronger appeal to the viewers?'

'Certainly it would,' said Czainski, 'and if you are willing, I will organize it so that you can practise with the band before we do the filming and recording – we have a recording studio on site. We need to get the ad ready as soon as possible so that it can go on air. Do you think you will need a lot of practice?'

'I doubt it,' said Anu. 'The tune is very familiar, and we're all used to singing – it'll be quite easy.'

The others nodded in agreement. They were thrilled!

'Gee, Uncle Jack,' said Amy, 'this is the most fantastic holiday I've ever had – thank you!'

The others chorused their thanks, too.

'You're more than welcome,' said Jack. 'Just watching all of you blossom, in so many ways, is as exciting as setting up a conservation.'

'Now, we'd better adjourn this meeting,' said Helen getting up. 'We have to get back to the site. I know you're all coming, but unfortunately, I have to rush off to a meeting – we have fifteen volunteers coming in at five, and they need to be briefed. Thanks again, folks. See you later!' She gave each of the children, and Hunter, a warm hug, and rushed off.

The youngsters collected their knapsacks, said goodbye to Aunty Meg and, piling into the various vehicles, went off to the site.

CHAPTER 14

A Very Stinky Rat

The tents were great! Set up close to the chalets on one side of the lake, the girls had a large blue tent, while the dark green tent for the boys was slightly smaller. After examining their tents and placing their knapsacks in them, the children changed into swimsuits and rushed over to Dolphin Bay as it was nearly time for their friends to arrive.

The DPs were delighted to see them, and said that they had worked out a programme in which Nimal, Hunter, Gina and Mich could do some stunts with the dolphins. The dolphins arrived, and everyone went into the water to play with them – including Hunter.

'What an inspiring experience,' said Amy later on, as they watched the dolphins swim off. 'I could play with them for ever. They make me feel quite . . . quite . . . *euphoric*!'

'I know exactly what you mean,' said Nimal. 'I can't wait to play with them again. Gina, Mich and I have to learn our roles, too – we'll be exceedingly clean beans, to say the least; by the end of each day, we'd have had at least four baths. And what a natural comedy team Hunter and Billy make!'

'By the way, folks,' said Chang, 'Jack asked if you four older ones would like to learn how to steer our motor boat. It's not as powerful as his, so Amy and Anu could have a go, too.'

'Cool!' said Rohan. 'Do we have time now?'

'Sure,' said Chang, 'it won't take long for you to learn – we could easily do an hour now – I'll take you out. Do you two want to come along for the ride?' he asked, turning to Gina and Mich.

'Of course,' they chanted, 'and Hunter as well.'

Waving goodbye to the other DPs, Chang, Hunter and the children swam out to the arms of the bay and clambered into the motor boat which was moored there.

In a short time the four older ones had mastered the basics and were able to start, steer and moor the boat with ease.

'Good work,' commented Chang. 'Tomorrow, I'll let you take it out on your own – it's quite safe in this area, and I know you'll be fine.'

They were thrilled. Rohan moored the boat and then, after thanking Chang, they walked back towards their tents, chatting eagerly about everything they'd done.

On the way, they met a group of people, ranging from sixteen to seventy years in age, all wearing bright blue T-shirts with the Conservation logo and 'Volunteer' printed on both the back and the front. They also wore name tags. Helen was taking them on a tour of the site, and she briefly stopped to greet the children.

'And these are the JEACs, including the dog,' said Helen with a smile. 'You'll hear more about them later on. JEACs, these are some of our volunteers who'll be working with us, learning how to direct and assist people when they visit the Conservation.'

As they greeted the volunteers, who were happy to meet them, Rohan noticed one man staring hard at him. He looked inquiringly at the man, noticing that his name was Alastair. However, Alastair merely nodded and the group moved on.

'Did you see that chap?' asked Rohan, as he and Nimal showered and changed. 'The big, hefty one, with a bald head?'

'Yeah,' said Nimal. 'He doesn't quite fit into the group somehow.'

'Exactimo!' said Rohan, thoughtfully. 'All the others looked friendly and keen. He looked morose and – I don't know – a total misfit. But I guess you shouldn't judge a book by its cover; who knows, perhaps he'll turn out to be the nicest of the lot.'

'Dream on, yaar,' said Nimal with a grin. 'What's happening this evening, do you know?'

'Other than the guards and us, I think everybody on site has a meeting after dinner – so I guess we're free till bedtime. What shall we do?'

'We haven't had a chance to visit the enclosure where the seal show takes place,' said Nimal, 'and I know Anu wanted to take a dekko so that we can get a sense of what props we need. It's exactly opposite our tents but we'd have to go right around the lake; we could walk there after dinner – what do you say?'

'Sure,' said Rohan, 'I don't think anyone will have a problem with that. Is that the pool enclosure where the seating is ready, and only the stage has to be completed?'

'Yeah,' said Nimal.

They joined the girls, who were chatting with Okanu.

'Have you had a chance to look over at least part of the Centre?' asked Okanu.

'Nope,' said Rohan, 'but we plan to do some exploring this evening. It's pretty humongous and we haven't had much free time so far.'

'True,' said Okanu. 'You've been working like beavers. Now, do you know where the most important building on the site is located?'

'Which building, Okanu?' queried Gina.

'The food hall, of course,' said Okanu, pretending to look shocked. 'Are you telling me you don't know where we eat?' He pointed to a large white chalet. 'That's where our kitchen staff resides and it has a huge dining room where we have our meals. Dinner is available from six onwards each evening, but Jack asked if you folk could meet him and Mike at 6:30 tonight, since we have a meeting at 7:30.'

'No problemo,' said Amy.

Okanu went off and Nimal looked at his watch.

'We have about half an hour; what shall we do?'

'Laze about near the lake?' suggested Amy.

'Mmmm . . . cool,' said Anu, walking towards the lake dreamily. 'What a view – the lake, trees, grass, perfume from the flowers, the salty taste in the air. Oh – I could live here forever!'

The others followed, chuckling at her whimsical air. Lying on the grass beside the lake, they drank in the beauty and listened to the soft sounds of the evening.

'What's that noise?' said Nimal suddenly, sitting up and looking around.

'What kind of noise?' said Gina. 'I can hear a sea lion.'

'No – listen,' said Nimal, standing up. 'Sounds like a helicopter.'

'You're right,' said Rohan, getting up to join Nimal. 'It's coming from that direction,' he continued, pointing towards the bay.

As the others stood up, they saw a small black seaplane fly over the far end of the Centre and turn towards the lake. Then they lost sight of it as it flew lower, behind the volcano and other buildings. But they could still hear it quite clearly.

'Perhaps it's going to land on the other side of the lake, near the volcano,' said Nimal. 'Maybe it's one of Uncle Jack's friends, but we can't see a thing from here. Let's run around. Wow – I'd love to get a closer view of a seaplane.'

But even as he said this, they saw the seaplane soar up into the sky again and fly back the way it came.

'Awesome,' said Rohan.

The boys discussed the plane as they walked back to the food hall, from which tantalizing aromas were emanating.

They served themselves and sat down to wait for the others.

'Did you have a good afternoon?' asked Mike, joining their table a few minutes later.

'It was splendiferous,' said Nimal, 'but, man, being in the open air makes me hungrier than ever! Okay, okay,' he continued with a grin as the others informed him that they didn't notice any difference in his appetite indoors or out. 'Perhaps it's just because I feel so energized after playing with the dolphins.'

Jack joined them, too, and they told him and Mike about their activities, including their lesson with Chang in the motor boat. The meal finished all too soon as Jack and Mike had to rush off for the meeting.

'Try and get to bed no later than ten,' said Jack. 'We start work around four in the morning, so you need some sleep. Have you got everything you need – will you be comfortable in the tents?'

'Of course, Uncle Jack,' said Rohan. 'Is it all right if we check out the seal show enclosure?'

'Sure,' said Jack. 'See you later.'

He hurried off. The JEACs and Hunter stopped at the girls' tent because Gina and Mich wanted to rollerblade.

'What a cosmopolitan crowd,' said Amy, watching adults hurrying to the meeting. 'I would love to work here.'

With Gina and Mich racing back and forth – Hunter running with them – they set off along the dimly lit pathway.

The seal enclosure was quite a distance away, but they strolled along, listening to the crickets chirruping in the grass and the frogs croaking in the lake.

'I feel like we own this place,' said Rohan with a laugh. 'Our kingdom! Not a soul in sight except for us.'

'Just look at the lake,' said Anu, 'smooth as glass, and the slides look like the humps of large monsters – listen – they're even growling.'

They laughed at her vivid imagination, but then, hearing the sputtering of an engine, stopped in their tracks, looking around to see where the noise was coming from.

'Sounds like that seaplane we heard earlier,' began Nimal, when, sure enough, it came into view, flying low over the Centre.

'Its skis look peculiar,' said Rohan, 'not as sleek as when we first saw it. Let's run round the track and see if we can watch it land.'

The boys sprinted ahead eagerly, the girls following slowly. They weren't that crazy about planes. As the boys rounded the curve of the lake they saw the plane skimming about a metre above the ground.

'Hey,' shouted Rohan above the noise, 'something's fallen off the skis.'

'It's two people,' said Nimal, squinting in the gloom. 'I bet they were lying on the skis. Did they fall off?'

'Hey, the plane's going off – that's bizarre,' exclaimed Rohan, as the plane pointed its nose skywards and flew away. 'There's something fishy going on,' he continued. 'Come on, yaar, let's check it out.'

'Those two went into the bushes,' said Nimal, who was straining to see in the dark. 'Why on earth would they jump off like that? Fishy's the word, yaar.'

'Girls – problem,' said Rohan, as Amy and Anu came up, followed by Mich, Gina and Hunter, seconds later. Explaining rapidly, Rohan asked them to contact the security guards at the gates and send someone to join them. 'You'd better take Hunter with you – and, hurry – stick together. Nimal and I'll see what's up.'

The girls raced off, while the boys ran towards the bushes into which Nimal had seen the figures disappear.

'I think they jumped off near the seal show enclosure,' panted Nimal.

The land sloped down towards the entrance to the enclosure; the boys searched the bushes but found no one. As they slid down the slope towards the enclosure – not waiting to get to the steps – they saw a spark of light, quickly followed by another spark.

'Is that a torch?' said Rohan.

'I'm not . . . oh, my hat – fire!' yelled Nimal, as flames suddenly shot up into the air.

'The stage – all that wood!' roared Rohan, sprinting towards the pool in the enclosure. He called over his shoulder, 'Nimal, break one of the fire alarms – quick – then let's try and put out the flames.'

Within minutes, Nimal set off the fire alarm and joined Rohan, who had found a couple of buckets. They set to work, trying to put out the fire which was quickly eating its way through the wood.

'It's spreading too fast,' gasped Rohan, who, like Nimal, was covered in soot. 'Where *are* the others?'

'I hear shouts,' puffed Nimal, 'help's on the way.'

In a few minutes there were staff members on the scene. Someone had driven the fire engine to the spot; buckets and fire extinguishers appeared like magic, and the fire was quickly doused. The boys, who had been working tirelessly, raised a cheer in which everyone joined. Jack, using a megaphone, requested that all staff, security and volunteers take a seat in the enclosure. The girls located Rohan and Nimal, and the JEACs stood together near the exit.

'Thanks for the hard work, folks,' began Jack. 'It looks a sorry sight but I don't think the damage is as bad as it might have been. We'll be able to fix it in time for OD. But what happened? Would you boys tell us what you know?'

Rohan and Nimal told them everything, starting from the point where they had seen the seaplane swoop down, and also mentioning that they had seen the same plane earlier in the evening.

'But we couldn't figure out where those two people disappeared to,' concluded Nimal. 'We searched the bushes thoroughly.'

'Well, this is a large conservation,' said Jack slowly, 'and they could be anywhere. It's easy enough to slip off in the dark. Let's break up into groups and search the place, and if we're unsuccessful, we'll call in the police. Okay – back to the office for torches, and make sure you have at least one mobile per group. We can't afford to have pyromaniacs running wild here.'

The crowd dispersed and made their way back to the office. The youngsters waited for Mike at the exit. As the volunteers were shepherded out of the enclosure by Helen, Rohan suddenly nudged Nimal and whispered.

'See that chap – the dark-haired one. He doesn't have the Conservation logo on his T-shirt, and except for the colour of his hair, he could easily be Don Ingram's twin.'

'Yeah,' breathed Nimal, staring hard at the boy. 'The features look the same. And the chap next to him could be his pal, George. But this guy has blond hair, and George's was brown – and there's no Conservation logo on his T-shirt either.'

'I smell a rat, yaar,' said Rohan softly. 'I don't remember them with the volunteers earlier on. Let's follow that group – we'll catch up with Mike later.'

Rohan quietly told the other JEACs about their suspicions.

'I think Helen said there were fifteen volunteers,' said Anu. 'Let's count them.'

'But some of them may have joined later or left early or something,' said Rohan. 'Anu, get Helen alone for a minute, and find out exactly how many volunteers there should be just now.'

Anu caught up with Helen, and after a brief conversation, reported back to the others.

'Fifteen,' she said.

'But there are seventeen,' whispered Gina. 'Mich and I both counted them.'

'Definitely a *very* stinky rat,' said Rohan. 'Do you think . . . no, surely they wouldn't be that bold? And even if they were, how on earth did they know when everyone was in a meeting and then get dropped off?'

'Talk *English*, Rohan,' begged Amy. 'What exactly are you saying?'

'Sorry, Amy,' said Rohan. 'I'm sure it is Don – he could be wearing a wig.'

'You're right on, Rohan,' said Anu. 'I've been observing the way he walks – with a distinctive swagger. I noticed that, both at the Big Pineapple and when he walked onto the stage at the campaign. And the other boy, George – his limp was identical to the way in which the other chap is limping.'

'Cheek!' exclaimed Amy, taking an impulsive step forward and being immediately pulled back by Rohan and Anu. 'Sorry – what should we do?'

'Wait till we reach the office. Mike, Okanu and Uncle Jack will be there, and then we'll confront the jerks,' said Rohan grimly. 'I just hope we're right!'

'I bet we are,' said Nimal. 'Gina and Mich, just hang on to Hunter for a bit.'

On reaching the office, some of the staff went inside to collect torches and mobiles. Jack, Mike and Okanu were giving out rapid instructions.

Rohan and Nimal, after a whispered conversation, moved towards the group of volunteers and managed to sneak up behind the two boys. Then, raising their hands simultaneously, they pulled hard at the suspects' hair, which came away in their hands, revealing Don and George.

An immediate hullabaloo broke out. Nimal grabbed George, who stayed quiescent, knowing he could not escape. Don, however, immediately and unexpectedly twisted out of Rohan's grip and, yelling abusively, tried to kick him.

Rohan dodged him easily, grabbed Don's arms again, and pinned them behind his back. All those who had been at the panel discussion recognized Don. Mike, Jack and Okanu reached the teens quickly.

'What are you boys doing here?' asked Jack quietly.

'None of your business,' said Don rudely. 'My father will get you – wait and see!' he shouted, swearing violently at Jack.

Before anyone could say a word, Nimal pushed George over to Okanu and stood in front of Don.

'Apologize!' growled the boy. 'Or would you like Rohan and me to teach you a lesson in good manners that you won't forget? You come here, set fire to the place and then try to sneak out – I'm sure the police will be very interested. Apologize to Uncle Jack, immediately.'

But despite the fact that he was in a nasty situation and could not escape repercussions, Don had lost his temper and was out of control. He spat at Nimal, and the staff roared with anger.

Don, past caring, swore obscenely and yelled, 'Oh, so he's your "uncle", is he? He should be kicked out, along with all of you – he and his crazy ideas. And then he brings people like you here to ruin my country.' He turned his head to glare at Rohan and said, 'Take your hands off me, and see if you have the guts to fight – I'm a karate champion!'

Jack and Mike, both red with anger, stepped forward, but Rohan spoke first and the men paused.

'So, you're a champion, huh?' said Rohan, softly. He swiftly twisted Don around to face him, and then released the teen. 'Well, champ, let's have a match.'

He bowed in the accepted manner for karate demonstrations but kept one eye on Don. Don didn't bother to bow.

Nimal stepped back and nobody interfered as Rohan and Don eyed each other warily. Rohan was as cool as a cucumber and didn't say a word, while Don swore at him.

Then Don charged towards Rohan and aimed another kick at him. He did not realize that Rohan was good at karate. Rohan grabbed his leg and, with one smooth move, threw him over his hip. Don landed heavily on the ground but was up in a jiffy.

'Lucky throw,' he snarled, but he was more careful this time as they circled, looking for an opening to attack.

The end came swiftly. Rohan darted towards Don and, before the boy could block him, felled him for the second time with a few quick chops. Don rose slowly, panting heavily. Rohan gave him no time to recover, but went in again, gripped Don's arm and threw him over his shoulder. This time Don lay on the ground, gasping, waiting for Rohan to kick him again.

Rohan dusted his hands together, gave him a look of loathing, and walked over to join Nimal.

The staff cheered, and Don was quickly collared by a couple of men.

Looking at Jack, Rohan said, half apologetically, 'He was begging for it, Uncle Jack. I'm positive he and George set fire to the place, and he has no right to abuse you, or anyone else.'

'I understand, Rohan,' said Jack soberly. 'I think we'll interrogate them ourselves, and if they won't tell us the truth, we'll call in the police.'

At the mention of the police, George started blubbering and despite Don's yells of 'Shut up, George,' he confessed that they had started the fire.

'Please don't put us in jail,' he begged. 'We'll never do anything like this again.'

There were angry murmurs from the staff. Jack, however, felt sorry for the weaker boy. He asked Mike, Okanu and Czainski to take the boys downtown, and drop them off near a telephone booth so that they could call their parents.

'I won't take it any further this time,' he said grimly, 'but if you ever come to this Conservation again, I'll personally make sure that you are handed over to the police.'

The men escorted the teens out to the cars, and took them away.

Helen saw the volunteers out of the Conservation. The staff agreed to pitch in and help clear up the charred wood from the enclosure, working in shifts so that everyone could get some rest; and Jack said he would join them once he had spoken with the JEACs.

He led the youngsters off to his chalet. Helen, Jalila and Padmini were there, too, and provided them with hot chocolate and biscuits, though no one felt like eating.

Jack thanked Rohan and Nimal for doing the majority of the work in putting out the fire. Then, smiling wryly, he said, 'Well, I'm impressed at your karate skills, Rohan, and at the way in which you turned a fight into a match. Don deserved what he got – and,' he added, collapsing into a chair and burying his head in his hands for a moment, 'if *you* hadn't taught him a lesson, Rohan, I would have!' He pretended to glare around.

Laughter dissolved the tension. There were hugs all round and Jack thanked the JEACs for helping to catch the culprits.

'Uncle Jack,' said Rohan, 'before you go – there's something very strange about this whole fiasco. How did these folks, presumably Ingram and Owen, since their sons were the pyromaniacs, know exactly when everyone would be in a meeting so that they could drop off the guys? There must be someone on the inside who's a traitor. I'm sure it can't be one of the staff – but a volunteer could get in fairly easily.'

'Hmmm . . . good point,' said Jack thoughtfully. He turned to the three women, 'I must go and help clear the debris. Perhaps first thing in the morning you three, together with Monique and Czainski, could go through the résumés of the volunteers carefully – particularly the ones who were here this evening. Though we don't want to accuse anyone unfairly – and we desperately need our volunteers – we should review our strategy for recruitment. What do you think?'

'Good idea,' said Helen. 'We'll check it out. This same group comes back the day after tomorrow for another orientation. I'll get back to you.'

'Can't we help clear up, too, Uncle Jack?' asked Amy, and the others all nodded eagerly.

'Thanks, folks,' said Jack warmly, smiling at the tired group. 'I think you would help best by going to bed – it's after midnight – and the recording is tomorrow. Don't worry, we're well organized. Now, I'd better go – goodnight, and thanks again.'

'You're welcome, Uncle Jack,' they chorused. Then, saying goodnight to the three ladies, they went off – to the showers first as they were still covered in soot, and then to their tents.

CHAPTER 15

Singing, Suspicions and Seals

'Where am I?' grunted Nimal the next morning, as he tried to roll over in the restrictive sleeping bag and got his face washed by Hunter.

'In a tent, yaar,' laughed Rohan, who was wide awake.

'I was dreaming of fires and karate fights all night!' said Nimal, tousling his hair.

'Me, too – and I feel like a cup of something hot,' said Rohan, getting out of his sleeping bag. 'Shall we mosey along to the food hall and see what's available?'

'Sure,' said Nimal, pushing away Hunter, who was trying to sit on him.

They showered and dressed rapidly. It was still fairly early in the morning, and Rohan glanced at the girls' tent.

'They're fast asleep – I don't see any movement,' he said. 'Come on, Hunter, let's go and find something to drink.'

The boys went to the hall, helped themselves to hot chocolate, gave Hunter a bowl of milk, and then moved over to a table near a window, where there was a plate of biscuits.

'Mmmm, that's good,' said Rohan, sipping his chocolate and helping himself to a biscuit. 'You remember that volunteer chappie, Nimal? The morose-looking one – Alastair.'

Just then Anu entered the room, got a glass of juice and joined the boys at their table. 'The others are still asleep,' she said. 'What's up? You look unusually serious.'

'That chap, Alastair,' said Rohan, 'I was asking Nimal if he remembered him.'

'Yeah, I do,' said Nimal. 'His face is indelibly printed on my memory since he looked so charming and friendly,' the boy continued, sarcastically.

'I noticed him, too,' said Anu. 'He looks like a good "bad" character for one of my books.'

'Well, I think we should keep an eye on him – he could be trouble,' said Rohan. As Nimal and Anu looked at him sharply, he continued, 'I think there's a traitor – it can't be any of the staff, they're too dedicated. So it *has* to be a volunteer. How else did Ingram and Co. know when to drop off those punks?'

'Yeah, I'm beginning to get a picture,' said Anu thoughtfully. 'This particular group of volunteers was here yesterday at the time of the fire. The jerks were wearing T-shirts identical to those worn by the volunteers, except that there were no logos on them. They may have hoped to sneak out of the gates with the volunteers, but we caught them. One of the volunteers could be involved, but he lay low when the boys were caught.'

'As logical as ever, sis,' said Rohan. 'But let's not jump to conclusions – go cautiously,' he added. 'We'll tell the others, too – I think there's a good possibility of it being Alastair and we'll keep an eye on him when he's here next.'

'Okay,' agreed Anu and Nimal.

'Here come the others, with Uncle Jack and Mike,' said Nimal. 'Let's not bother them with our ideas. They've got enough on their plates just now, and we may be quite wrong.'

Rohan and Anu nodded and the three of them went over to greet the others.

'Brekker's up,' said Amy. 'You're early birds – have you been here long?'

'Not too long,' said Anu smiling. 'I still have a yawn or two left in me.'

'What time's the recording?' asked Amy

'In 45 minutes,' said Jack. 'How do you folks feel this morning? Up to it?'

'No problemo, Uncle Jack,' said Gina.

As they sat down to breakfast, Jack and Mike updated them about the fire. Fortunately, not too much damage had been caused and the enclosure would still be ready by the end of the week.

Helen joined them and said, as she bent down to pat Hunter, 'Gina, Mich and Hunter, could you please come and see me in my office today, after lunch? I have your knapsacks ready and we have some deliveries for you.'

'Yippee!' chorused the girls, 'We'll be there, Helen!'

'Had enough to eat?' queried Jack. As they nodded, he said, 'Let's go over to the office building – the band's there, and Monique and Czainski will supervise the recording.'

Walking towards the administrative buildings, Jack continued, 'We'd also like Hunter to join your group. At the end of the song the cameras will focus on you youngsters – you'll stand in front of the first picture and we'd like Hunter to bark and shake paws with each of you. Then, all of you say, "Join us, please – especially on the twenty-second of December!" and point at the picture, which will have the name of our Conservation and the date of the inauguration.'

'That's a great conclusion,' said Anu.

'When will it be on TV?' asked Mich eagerly.

'This evening – the first ad will run on Channel 17 at 8 o'clock,' said Mike, 'and after that, three other TV channels, and five cable channels, are picking it up and will air it hourly. It will also be on six of the popular radio stations. Make sure you meet in Jack's chalet just before eight, to watch the first run, okay?'

'Wouldn't miss it for the world,' said Rohan. 'An ad – by our two famous sisters – and a super one at that!'

The younger girls giggled, but were thrilled all the same – praise from Rohan meant more to them than praise from any adult.

The recording studio was huge and the technical team was nearly ready to begin. Monique and Czainski greeted the JEACs and introduced them to the director of operations. Wires were running all over the room, and a small stage had been set up at one end, with a large screen in the middle. The picture, with the name of the Centre, was already on the screen. It had been enlarged and the colours softened, so that it made a beautiful background. The children watched the activity with interest. Just behind the first stage was a second one, connected to it by a ramp. It was larger and there was a beautiful drum set on it.

A few minutes later, a group of four adults walked in, three of them carrying guitars. They came over to the JEACs, and the tallest man, who was over six feet, introduced himself as Rob and asked if he could shake the hands of the two famous people who had put together that wonderful advertisement. Nimal pointed to Mich and Gina.

Rob, bowing low, said in a bass voice that seemed to come up from his boots, 'So you're the stars – do you mind giving me your autographs, please? On my T-shirt would be fine.'

Gina and Mich giggled shyly, and shook their heads. Rob grinned, shook hands with all of them and with Hunter, too, and introduced his band: Ginger – a short man with bright red hair; Jackie – blonde and petite; and Gertie – a contralto who could make the funniest faces.

'We're known as the Frolicsome Four or FF for short,' said Ginger sadly, 'at least, I *think* that's our name,' he added with a worried frown, trying to squint down the back of his T-shirt, and falling over in the attempt.

'You're quite right,' said Gertie, helping him up and turning him around so that the JEACs could read what was written on his T-shirt. 'Cheer up, love,' she said consolingly as Ginger pretended to burst into tears at his forgetfulness. 'You got the name right this time.'

The FF explained that they had their own children's TV show and also sang as a band. They would be at the Conservation on OD, since they were passionate conservationists, and had asked Jack if he would let them provide the live music for that day – on a volunteer basis.

The director then asked for everyone's attention, and serious work began, interspersed, naturally, with much laughter and frivolity. The band was fabulous, and worked well with the JEACs – who all sang the main tune, while the FF provided the harmony. As Rob said, after a few rehearsals and a trial recording, 'If I say so meself, it sounds very professional.'

By 1 p.m. the final recording was pronounced perfect. Hunter performed excellently, waving a paw and barking loudly at the end of the advertisement.

Jack, Mike and Helen joined the group to view the finished piece.

'Fantastic job,' said Jack, beaming at them all and giving Hunter a big hug. 'Congratulations, folks, and thanks for being so generous with your time and talents.'

'You're welcome, Jack,' said Rob.

'Come and join us for lunch,' said Mike, issuing a general invitation to everyone present.

'Thanks, Mike,' said the director, speaking for the recording team, 'but we've got tons of work to do before this will be ready to go on air. We'll get some sandwiches from the kitchen.'

'Too bad, mate,' said Ginger, looking at the director and wincing in pain. 'You could do with more than sandwiches – I can barely see you sideways.'

Laughing at his nonsense, because the director was a large man, the JEACs said goodbye and went to the food hall with the Frolicsome Four.

After a riotous lunch, the FF had to leave, and the JEACs said goodbye to them reluctantly, cheering up at the reminder that they would see them again on OD.

The afternoon flew by. Gina, Mich and Hunter were feeling very important indeed. They each had a blue knapsack with pictures of dolphins and other sea creatures on it, which read 'AFC&DB Special Courier'.

There were plenty of deliveries, and Helen, Monique, Joe and Malika kept them busy. Hunter joined the girls on most of their runs – but occasionally he was sent on a run by himself, to find and make a delivery to Mike, Jack, Anu, or one of the older JEACs. By 6:30 p.m. the youngsters, and Hunter, were bushed, and collapsed on the grass in front of their tent – all of them panting.

The four older ones were already seated there, and laughed at their flushed faces. Anu got them something to drink, and they lolled around on the grass before dinner, discussing their day. Nimal and Anu had done a lot of work with the seals and actors, and the next day they would need Hunter for a short time, so that he could learn his part and make friends with the baby seals.

'He's already friends with the bigger seals,' said Nimal, patting the dog. 'I introduced him to them, and the attraction was mutual.'

Rohan and Amy were pleased at the way the waterskiing programme was developing. Rohan had ridden a jet ski for the first time, and was thrilled with the powerful machine.

The four older ones had also taken the motor boat out on their own, and were now quite comfortable handling it.

'Nimal,' said Rohan, 'tell Amy, Gina and Mich about Alastair.'

'Oh, yeah,' said Nimal.

He quickly told them of their suspicions and warned them to look out for anything unusual that Alastair might do.

'Such as what, Nimal?' asked Gina. 'Do you think he'll try to burn down something else?'

'I really don't know, Gina,' said Nimal. 'But if you see him going off on his own, let us know immediately.'

'Okay,' said Mich and Gina.

'Isn't it dinner time yet?' asked Gina plaintively. 'I'm simply *starving*!'

'Wretch,' said Nimal, lazily reaching out to tumble her in the grass, but the little girl got out of his reach quickly.

'Aren't you JEACs hungry tonight?' called a voice, and Okanu appeared from behind the tent.

'Starving!' yelled Mich and Gina, and they raced ahead of the others to the food hall.

'Early bed for all of you,' said Mike, as they joined him at a table with Monique and Helen. 'I saw you smother a yawn, Nimal.'

'I sure don't mind an early night,' said Rohan. 'I feel like I've been fighting to control that jet ski all day. Man – it sure is powerful, and my muscles are pretty sore.'

'I'll give you some Deep Heat to ease your muscles, yaar,' said Mike.

'Thanks,' said Rohan. 'By the way, where's Uncle Jack?'

'He and Czainski are at a dinner meeting with some of the news folk,' said Monique. 'They have a press conference tomorrow morning. Now, let's hurry so that we can watch the first run of the ad.'

They gobbled up their food, and rushed over to Jack's place. Ten minutes later they were watching themselves on TV.

'Wow, I can't believe we actually did that,' said Gina, at the end of the advertisement. She looked slightly bemused.

'It's terrific,' said Monique.

'It's fantastic! Now, bedtime, JEACs,' said Mike, shooing them off, and handing Rohan the Deep Heat.

'What time do we start tomorrow?' yawned Rohan, as he and Nimal cuddled into their sleeping bags, Hunter lying down between them.

'Helen wants to meet us at 8:30, before the volunteers turn up,' said Nimal. 'Go to sleep, yaar – I'll set my alarm for five and we can jog around the Centre a couple of times, before the others are up . . . might loosen your muscles before you have to ride that jet ski again.'

'Good idea,' said Rohan. 'The Deep Heat's kicking in.' He turned over and was asleep within minutes.

Nimal read for a while and then went to sleep, too.

They awoke early, feeling refreshed, though Rohan groaned a bit as he got out of his sleeping bag. However, after a few stretching exercises he was ready for a jog, and the boys and Hunter set off.

It was a gorgeous morning; the sky was a pale blue with tiny white clouds drifting lazily along. The boys paused at Dolphin Bay to watch a spectacular sunrise, and then jogged back to the tent.

It was still early by the time they emerged from their showers and dressed, so they strolled along to the food hall and had a hearty breakfast.

By 8:30 the JEACs were assembled in Helen's office, ready for another busy day. Helen quickly went over their responsibilities, checking to see that they were not experiencing any problems, and praising them for their hard work. Then she bustled off, taking Gina, Mich and Hunter with her, as some deliveries were already required.

The four older ones stopped to chat with Joe and Malika, and then dispersed, waving to the 'Speedy Trio', as they had named the little couriers, who whizzed past them to make their deliveries.

Rohan and Amy practised with the waterskiers for an hour, while Nimal and Anu worked on the seal show. Then all of them worked and played with the dolphins; Aneeka, Chang and Jane were not feeling well and had asked if Rohan, Anu and Amy could lend a hand. After a hectic but satisfying morning, they gathered for lunch, and saw the volunteers seated at a table with Helen, Joe and Malika. They waved to them, but joined Monique and Jalila at another table.

Rohan and Nimal were facing the volunteers, and Rohan noticed that Alastair looked over at their table frequently. He nudged Nimal, drawing his attention to this. However, whenever Nimal and Rohan looked at Alastair, he avoided eye contact.

Following the meal, by silent consent, the boys walked over to Alastair's table and, after the usual preliminary 'hellos' and 'how are things going', Rohan spoke to Helen and asked her when she would be free that evening as they needed to meet with her.

'I know you're tied up with the volunteers,' said Rohan, smiling charmingly at all of them, 'so, perhaps, when they leave? What time will that be?'

'Oh – we'll be finished here by six,' said a pretty blonde girl of eighteen, before Helen could say a word. 'Wish we could stay on longer,' she continued, fluttering her long eyelashes at Rohan, who was, as far as she was concerned, her ideal hero – handsome, athletic and able to conquer bad guys, like Don, with ease.

'Er . . .' stammered Rohan, turning red, taken aback by her blatant admiration.

'Six will be fine for a meeting then, Helen,' said Nimal, hiding a grin at Rohan's embarrassment. 'If that's all right with you?'

'Sure boys,' said Helen, smiling widely at them, and winking at Nimal.

'Come on, Rohan, the girls are waiting,' said Nimal, and smiling politely at everyone, the boys went over to join the others who were waiting for them at the door.

'Your face! If only you could see your face,' gasped Nimal, the second they were outside. 'A tomato couldn't have been redder!'

Rohan made a swipe at him, still slightly crimson in the face, and, of course, the girls wanted to know what had happened. Nimal told the tale, exaggerating it to the extent that Amy and the younger girls quite believed that Rohan had spoken exclusively to the pretty volunteer, and was going on a date with her at six.

'Come off it, Nimal,' said Anu, reading the look on Amy's face, and giving him a quick punch. 'Tell the truth, for once!'

Rohan threatened to annihilate him, so Nimal sobered up and told the truth. 'But that's what *always* happens,' he continued, grinning wickedly and quickly moving out of Rohan's reach. 'All the girls fall for him because he's so *cute!*'

'I'll "cute" you,' growled Rohan, and they promptly had a mock karate fight in which Rohan was the easy victor, and Nimal had to take back the word 'cute'.

'Did you notice Alastair staring at us when we were at their table?' asked Nimal, when they reached the tents and relaxed on the grass for a while. The little girls and Hunter had rushed back to the office to make more deliveries.

'Sure did,' said Rohan, who had recovered his aplomb. 'He was listening intently, but wouldn't meet my eye when I deliberately looked at him. And did you notice he was carrying a mobile?'

'Well, most people carry mobiles these days,' said Anu thoughtfully. 'I wish we knew whether he's really a bad guy or just *looks* menacing. He sure doesn't look appealing from a distance.'

'He's even less appealing, close-up,' said Rohan.

'Definitely not as pretty as the blonde beauty, is he?' teased Nimal.

'I prefer long dark hair,' said Rohan deliberately, getting up and stretching as he looked across the lake.

Only Anu noticed that Amy immediately looked happier although she said nothing. The girl had been extremely quiet while Nimal was teasing Rohan. 'I must talk to Nimal,' said Anu to herself. 'As for Rohan – he's a cool fish!'

Bickering amicably, the four of them went off to the seal enclosure. It being too hot for Rohan and Amy to do any of their tasks, Anu asked them to join Nimal and her to give them constructive feedback on the seal show. Falling behind Rohan and Amy for a few minutes, Anu spoke firmly to Nimal, who listened to her in astonishment.

'And you're not to tease either of them,' scolded Anu, looking at his mischievous face.

'But do you think he likes her – I mean – in a special way?' queried Nimal, not quite able to see his cousin as having a potentially serious girlfriend.

'I'm not sure,' said Anu. 'But I've never seen Rohan this comfortable before, so just leave them alone. Who knows what'll happen. Now, promise you won't bug them.'

'Okay, Aunty – you sometimes have a bizarre sixth sense about others,' said Nimal. 'You know I always do as you say.'

'Huh! Like fun, you do,' said Anu scathingly, as they caught up with Rohan and Amy.

'When's Hunter going to make friends with the seal pups?' asked Amy, who was her usual chatty self once again.

'Gina and Mich will bring him along in an hour and we'll see how he and the babies react to each other,' said Nimal.

The show was fun, and Rohan and Amy thoroughly enjoyed it. They had no criticism to offer, and the seal pups were adorable.

When Hunter and the younger girls joined them, the others sat back and watched Nimal work with the dog and the baby seals.

Nimal first fussed over Hunter, talking to him softly and lovingly. Then he made him sit down while he went over to the little pond where the pups were sporting in the water, and let them out of their enclosure. They immediately rushed over to the boy, rubbing their soft noses on any part of his body they could reach, and barking in their high-pitched little voices.

Nimal, the babies following him in a line – just like school children out on a walk with their teacher – went back towards Hunter. Nimal sat down a few metres away from the dog, and the seal pups were all over him in a moment. But, with a gesture, he made them sit in a row – they had learned a lot from their practices for the show.

'Hunter – come here, boy,' called Nimal quietly.

The dog obeyed immediately, and sat next to him, staring at the baby seals. He thought they might be puppies, since they barked, too, but they smelt fishy.

'Friends, Hunter,' said Nimal, picking up a baby seal and holding it on his lap.

The pup was not at all scared of Hunter, and put its little face close to the dog, who, though he backed away rapidly at first, came back at Nimal's request, and sniffed at the seal. Then he sat down, put out his paw to touch it, and barked at it very softly. Nimal moved away slowly, and as the others watched in delight, the four baby seals surrounded Hunter, and whenever he barked, they barked back.

'They're having a conversation,' exclaimed Jalila, clapping her hands in delight.

The baby seals, hearing the clapping sound, immediately clapped their flippers together, too – as they had been learning to do at the practices – and looked up for the fish they knew they would receive.

Nimal immediately threw each of them the fish they richly deserved, and gave Hunter a large biscuit as a reward.

'It'll be superfantabulous,' cried Amy ecstatically. She was thrilled with the baby seals. 'Can we cuddle them, too, Nimal?'

'Sure, come on over,' said Nimal. 'They're friendly pups – but you'd better put on some overalls first, or you'll smell distinctly fishy.'

After much cuddling of the babies, they had another rehearsal of the show, Gina and Mich seeing it for the first time. It went off splendidly, Hunter and the pups adding natural comedy to the story.

'We've got to go back now,' said Gina, 'but Hunter can stay and practise some more.'

She and Mich darted off. Rohan and Amy watched a couple more rehearsals, and then Hunter and the four of them strolled over to the office where Joe and Malika had a few desk jobs for them – sending out faxes, emails, photocopying, et cetera.

'Jack said Aunty Meg was coming to the site for a couple of days. She misses all of you so much that she wants to join the fun,' said Joe.

'Goody,' said Nimal, busy collating copies. 'We miss her, too.'

They saw Gina and Mich at intervals as they came rushing back to collect and make more deliveries around the Centre. Hunter stayed with the teens.

'Tea time – though a rather late one – it's 5:15,' said Joe. 'You folks have been great, thanks. Why don't you take a break and we'll join you shortly.'

'Right – see you later,' said the teens.

'I wonder where the girls are?' said Anu, as they entered the food hall and saw no sign of Gina and Mich.

'The last delivery I heard Malika give them was to Helen,' said Amy. 'They're probably having tea with her in one of the little cafes which were being set up today.'

'Oh – right,' said Anu, 'they seem to be having a great time. Here you go, Hunter – milk and biscuits.'

Hunter gobbled it up hungrily.

CHAPTER 16

Where Can They Be?

After tea the teens sat where they could see the gates to the Centre, and at six they saw Helen shepherd the volunteers out.

They strolled towards the office, and a few minutes later Helen joined them in the conference room.

'Where are Gina and Mich – aren't they coming to this meeting?' asked Helen, collapsing into a comfortable chair and removing her shoes. 'Oooh – my feet are killing me.'

'Yeah, but we thought they'd come with you,' said Anu. 'Didn't you see them at tea time?'

'Well, the last I saw of them was around five, when they delivered some papers to me at the cafe where we were having tea,' said Helen. 'Then I went over to talk to Okanu. The girls were chatting to the volunteers who must have given them some tea. Check with Joe and Malika and see if they were sent on more deliveries after that.'

Rohan checked but returned to say, 'Malika says that the delivery to you was the last one she gave the girls. Neither she nor Joe have seen them since.'

'They must be somewhere on the Conservation,' said Anu, 'though it's unlike them not to join us as soon as they're free.'

'Maybe they forgot the meeting and went off to chat with the DPs,' said Nimal. 'You know how they love the dolphins. We'll check there.'

'Good idea,' said Rohan, getting up immediately. 'I'm sure they're fine, but let's double-check.'

'Yes, please do,' said Helen. 'Hold on – let's see if I can reach Ian on his mobile.' She dialled the number but received no response. 'Here,' she said, handing Rohan a spare mobile, 'take this with you, and as soon as you check with the DPs, let me know, okay? Ian has a mobile but they don't always have it handy.'

'Sure, Helen,' said Rohan. He and the others hurried over to Dolphin Bay, getting there in record time.

'No, I haven't seen the kiddies this evening,' said Ian, who was the only one there. He had not turned his mobile phone on after the last practice. 'I saw them at the afternoon practice, but since the other three DPs are pretty sick, and in bed, I told the girls and Nimal to keep away as they couldn't afford to fall sick, too. Do you think something's happened to the kiddies?'

'I hope not,' said Rohan, 'But . . .' his voice trailed away anxiously.

'It's seven now,' said Nimal, concern sharpening his voice.

'Let's call Helen,' said Amy.

'Okay.' Rohan dialled the number. 'Helen? It's Rohan – the DPs haven't seen the girls either. What next?'

'Come right back to the office, and tell Ian to keep his mobile turned on,' said Helen abruptly.

'Will do,' said Rohan and rang off.

He passed on Helen's message to Ian, and then the teens and Hunter ran back to the office.

'Right,' said Helen, 'let's not panic. The rest of the Management Team is on its way here. I've checked with a few folk – they haven't seen the girls recently, either. What news, Joe?'

'Nothing from the food hall, Helen,' said Joe, coming in with Malika. 'The staff last saw the girls around 4:30, when they refilled their bottles of water and juice. I asked some of them to check the tents and chalets to see if the girls have fallen asleep, or are chatting to someone. I should hear back soon.'

'We're also calling all the shops and restaurants to determine if anyone saw them after five,' said Malika.

They returned to the telephones, leaving the others in the conference room to rack their brains as to where the little girls might have gone. Mike and the others arrived just as Joe returned to say that no one had seen the girls after five.

'Right – let's make an announcement over the PA system, asking all sections to call in and report that they have *not* seen the girls,' said Mike. 'Monique, would you do that, please? And ask them to call not only the main office lines but any of our mobiles if the lines are busy. Say it's a high priority call. Keep some staff lists handy – we'll check off to ensure that everyone has called in before we take the next step.'

Monique bustled off and a few minutes later they heard her voice over the PA system. She had barely finished her announcement when internal lines and mobile phones started ringing. Within fifteen minutes everyone had called in; no one had seen the girls after five.

'I'm going to call Jack,' said Mike, trying to keep the concern out of his voice. 'I'm sure the girls are okay, but I know he would prefer to know what's happening.'

He went to his office to call Jack. A few minutes later, he transferred the call to the conference room, asking Helen to put it on speakerphone.

'Hello,' came Jack's calm voice over the speaker, 'let's commence a search immediately – Mike will take charge of that. We need folk in the office – anyone who has information should report to the office and it can be announced over the PA system. Rohan, Anu, Amy and Nimal – I know you'll want to join the search parties, too, and that's fine. But all of you, and Hunter, please stay together. I'll be there shortly, with Aunty Meg. Don't panic – it won't help logical thought.'

He rang off. Mike organized things quickly and the adults left the office, going in various directions to set up search parties. The JEACs looked at each other.

'Where shall we search?' asked Anu.

'Let's first check with the security guard at the gates and see if he saw them leaving the Centre,' ventured Rohan.

'Good idea,' said Nimal.

They set off.

'But why would they have gone *outside* the Centre, Rohan?' asked Amy anxiously.

'I don't know,' said Rohan thoughtfully, 'it's just a hunch – but I have a nasty feeling about this. The girls always join us as soon as they're free.'

'Yeah,' agreed Nimal, 'and if one of them had been injured or something, the other would have come for help.'

'Also, the office folk would never send them into danger,' said Anu. 'Ah, hello, Bhopinder,' she greeted the guard, as they reached him.

'Hi,' said Bhopinder. 'This is very worrying about the little girls – have you got any news?'

They told him about the search parties.

'Bhopinder, you didn't by any chance see them go out of the gates, did you?' said Nimal.

'No,' said Bhopinder. 'I'd have stopped them if they were on their own.'

'Were you at the gates the whole time?' asked Rohan. 'What happens if you need a break? I hope you don't mind us asking all these questions, Bhopinder. We're just trying to figure out what could have happened.'

'No, of course I don't mind, Rohan,' said Bhopinder. 'Yes, I was at the gates all day, and when I need a break, I call one of the other workers to take my place.'

'The girls couldn't possibly have gone out then . . .' began Anu.

'Wait!' exclaimed Bhopinder, interrupting her. 'There was a period of about ten minutes, when I was helping a large truck to reverse, and at that time I couldn't see the gates. But that's quite a long shot, isn't it?'

'You can't tell. What time was that?' asked Rohan.

'Around 5:15 or so,' said Bhopinder.

'Whose truck was it?' asked Nimal.

'The Mowgli Catering truck. They were making a delivery to one of the restaurants.'

'They might have seen something,' said Rohan. 'Thanks, Bhopinder – we'll ask Helen to call them, and let you know if we come up with anything. See you.'

They ran back to the office and Helen immediately called the caterers, putting the telephone on speaker once more.

'Yes, madam, we did have a truck there this evening, with two of our staff and the driver,' said the manager. 'I'll put Hamish on – he was one of the men with the truck.'

'Good evening, madam,' said Hamish, seconds later, 'how may I help you?'

'We just wondered if, as you were leaving our premises, you saw two little girls on rollerblades?' said Helen. 'Both of them are nine years old, and have short, curly hair – one ash-blonde and the other black.'

'Oh, yes, madam,' said Hamish immediately. 'I saw them at the gate and waved – they waved back.'

'Where were they going? Did you see?' asked Helen eagerly.

'They went out into the car park and round the corner, madam. I was at the gate, and did not see them get into a car or anything like that. I assumed that their parents must be waiting for them in the other car park – I know there's one on the other side. Why, is something wrong?'

'Well, the children belong to us and they've been missing since that time. You're the first person to give us any information about them, Hamish. Thanks very much for your help.'

'Oh – I'm really sorry, madam. If I can be of any more assistance, please call me.'

'We will, Hamish,' said Helen. She rang off and looked at the teens, who were already at the door.

'It doesn't make any sense,' said Helen, 'but once you've checked out the car park, come right back.'

They nodded and ran off. Stopping only to brief Bhopinder about what Hamish had said, they went towards the car park.

'Here we are,' said Rohan, turning the corner into the large car park on one side of the Conservation.

'None of the staff or volunteers park in this area,' said Amy.

'I wonder . . . hmmm . . . let's look around anyway,' said Rohan. 'I have a vague idea. Let's see if we can spot anything unusual – something Gina or Mich might have dropped.'

'Okay,' said Anu.

They split up and searched the entire parking lot, which was well lit.

'Look! See what I've found,' exclaimed Rohan, who was searching a far corner.

The others ran over, and he pointed to a damp black spot on the ground. 'I think it's petrol,' he said, squatting on the ground to sniff at it. 'It certainly smells like it. Nimal?'

'Petrol all right,' said Nimal, wrinkling his nose. 'But anyone could have parked here and their car may have leaked.'

'Yeah, but let's look around this area, anyway,' said Anu.

'Gee whizz – look,' said Amy, a few minutes later. She showed them what she had found – it was a little blue bow – the kind Gina wore on a clip in her hair. 'I found this in the grass just beyond the gas spill – I'm sure the girls were here.' She continued, 'But why? Why would they come out here in the first place and, secondly, why would Gina throw away her bow? I know they're firmly fixed and can't just fall off.'

'She might have thrown it out of a car window if they had been kidnapped and she wanted to give us a clue,' said Anu.

'Kidnapped!' exclaimed Amy, staring at Anu and turning pale. 'Why would anyone kidnap the girls?'

'To blackmail Uncle Jack,' said Rohan grimly. 'I'm sure the Ingrams are behind this. Come on – let's go back. We'll have to involve the police.'

As they reached the gates, Jack drove in and they waited for him and Aunty Meg to join them.

'We've discovered something, Uncle Jack,' said Rohan. 'Let's go to the conference room.'

Once everyone was gathered together, Jack looked at the youngsters and said, 'Spill the beans, folks.'

Rohan quickly updated them and concluded by saying, 'I'm almost sure we won't find the girls on the Conservation.'

'Right – kidnapping sounds plausible,' said Jack thoughtfully. 'I have a good friend in the police department and I'll contact him immediately. In the meantime – it's now nine, let's do a general check to see if anyone in the Centre has further news. Monique – could you make another announcement over the PA system, please?'

Monique and Jack went off. Within minutes mobiles and telephones started ringing again – no one had good news.

'Rajiv, my friend in the police force, says it's best to wait and see if we get a call or a note from the kidnappers,' said Jack, coming back to the conference room. 'He'll be here shortly, along with his team and the necessary equipment to trace calls. Joe, Malika – I know you'll assist them in every way possible. Monique – please request key staff to meet in the food hall immediately,' said Jack.

Once they were assembled in the food hall, over a quick meal, which Jack insisted they eat, he updated the staff on the situation.

Hunter, meanwhile, was puzzled and could not figure out where the little girls were. He kept going to the door of whichever room the teens were in, and looking out to see if the girls were coming.

'I wish Hunter had been with them,' groaned Nimal, trying to force food down his throat. 'He wouldn't have let anyone kidnap them.'

'We'll find them, don't worry,' said Mike gruffly. 'Remember last year, how you youngsters got out of a bad situation? I'm sure the girls will be back soon.'

'But . . . if it's those horrible Ingrams – they may hurt them,' said Amy, gritting her teeth.

'They wouldn't dare,' said Jack gently. 'They know they'll go to jail for the rest of their lives if anything happens to the children. And now, the four of you, please return to your tent and do some brainstorming.'

'Can't we do that in one of the offices, Uncle Jack?' pleaded Rohan. 'Then we'll be on the spot if a call comes through.'

'Sure,' said Jack. 'Use one of the conference rooms.'

In the conference room they looked at each other anxiously. Their younger sisters were possibly in the hands of kidnappers – what would happen to them?

'Okay,' said Rohan, taking a deep breath. 'Let's try and think logically. Why would the girls have gone out of the gates in the first place?'

'Because they were asked to deliver something to someone,' said Anu promptly.

'But by whom, and to whom?' questioned Rohan. 'None of the staff gave them any deliveries after five, and in any case, they wouldn't have given them a delivery outside the gates – that leaves the volunteers.'

As Anu, Nimal and Amy stared at him he continued.

'Well, if a volunteer asked them to deliver a package to somebody outside the gates, in the further car park for instance, the girls would naturally do that – no questions asked. Of course, if Helen were there, she would have stopped them. But Helen said she last saw them at five, before she went over to Okanu. The caterers saw them around 5:15, *going out through the gates.* So – the last people to talk to the girls were the volunteers.'

'Good thinking, Rohan,' said Nimal. 'Carry on.'

'I wouldn't be surprised if it was Alastair,' continued Rohan. 'He may have had accomplices outside, in the car park – in a car which had a petrol leak,' he concluded excitedly, 'and they drove off with the girls. I think we should call the volunteers and check.'

'And Gina must have rolled down the window and thrown out the bow from her hair,' said Nimal, thumping the table in his eagerness. 'Smart kid – I bet she had her wits about her!'

'But if they were able to roll down the window,' said Amy, 'why didn't they open the car doors and get out?'

'Probably because the car was moving and the kidnappers activated the childproof locks; but Gina was able to roll down a window, at least for a few seconds,' said Rohan.

'It makes sense,' said Anu. 'I guess the next step is to ask Helen to call the volunteers. I'll go and get her.'

She returned with Helen who immediately called Agnes, one of the volunteers.

'Agnes? Sorry to call you so late,' said Helen, 'but our little girls are missing. The last time they were seen here was around five – when they were having tea with all of you.' She paused and then said, 'Thanks so much, Agnes – I'll call Boris right away. Bye for now.'

She rang off and said to the teens, as she hunted through her list for another number, 'Agnes said Boris was talking to the girls over tea – they were at the same table, and he might know where they went next. I'll put him on speaker.'

She soon had Boris on the line. 'Hello, Boris – it's Helen MacDonald – from the Conservation. Sorry to disturb you so late at night.'

'No problem, Helen,' said a sleepy voice over the speakerphone. 'What's up?'

Helen explained briefly and Boris immediately said, in a much more alert tone, 'But yes – the children were at a table with Marnie, Alastair and me. We gave them some tea.'

'Then what?' prompted Helen.

'Well, Alastair told the girls that you wanted them to deliver two packages to a friend. The friend had a dark blue car and would be parked in the car park on the other side of the Conservation. So the children thanked us for the tea, took the packages from Alastair, and went off. Such nice kids . . . but do you mean to say they're missing?'

'No time for more details, Boris,' said Helen grimly, 'but yes, the girls can't be found. Also, I didn't request any deliveries outside the gates.

You've been most helpful, but I have to run – oh – just a minute . . . hang on.'

She listened to Rohan, who had signalled her urgently, and then spoke into the telephone again, 'By the way, Boris, do you know much about Alastair?'

'Not really, Helen,' said Boris. 'Actually, this is the first time I've met him and he doesn't mix much or talk to any of us. Between you and me, none of us really like him – he's a very dour man.'

'Thanks again, Boris,' said Helen. 'Call the office any time – someone will be able to update you. Bye.' She rang off and turned to the teens saying, 'I think your hunches have paid off. I'm going to call Jack, who's with Rajiv, and we'll see if the police can find Alastair. We have an address for him.'

She bustled off, leaving the children talking excitedly.

'They may have an address for him,' said Rohan, 'but it's probably false. I think they should question the staff at Ingram's lodge, and see if there's anyone named Alastair on staff.'

'Brainwave, yaar!' said Nimal. 'Let's tell Mike and see what he says – Uncle Jack's too busy.'

'Call him on his mobile,' said Amy, whose mind was beginning to come up with ideas, too, instead of just questions. She had never before been involved in an adventure like this.

'Good thinking, Amy,' said Rohan, rapidly dialling Mike's number, and putting the call on speakerphone. 'Mike? It's Rohan. We've got news.'

He quickly told Mike about the latest developments and had just finished when Jack and Helen came in with the police officer.

'It's Mike,' whispered Anu to Jack.

'Good – stay on the line, Mike,' said Jack. 'We have more news. I just received a call from the telegraph office with an urgent telegram for me – from someone named Mojo. It said, "We have the two little girls – they are safe and will not be harmed if you promise to give us five million dollars. Signal your acceptance by flying white flags around Dolphin Bay at 6 p.m. tomorrow and the little girls will be returned – once we receive the money. When we see the flags we will send you instructions as to where you should leave the money and how you can find the girls." And that's all the telegram said.'

'Apparently,' continued Rajiv, 'they didn't call the telegraph office – someone pushed the note under the office door and disappeared by the time the staff went out to see who had delivered it.'

'But . . . why on earth would they kidnap the children?' asked Aunty Meg.

'They know we don't have enough money to both pay a ransom of five million dollars, and also go ahead with the opening of the Centre,' said Jack wearily. 'They're trying to obstruct us again and they sure have picked a good way to do it – I don't know if anyone has the heart to put money into the Conservation until, and unless, the girls are found safely.'

'Jack,' said Rajiv, 'from all I've heard, I'm positive Ingram is behind this, and the first thing we need to do is to check up on Alastair and find out his connection to Ingram. Then we'll twist Ingram's arm and see what information we can scare out of him. If this chap is the same Alastair – one of Ingram's men – we've come across him before. He and a guy called Eugene are two nasty characters.'

'Eugene?' said Amy. 'A member of Ingram's team at the campaign was called Eugene.'

'Great! We'll check that, too,' said Rajiv. 'Also, can anyone describe Alastair?'

'I'll draw you a picture,' said Nimal at once, and set to work with a pencil and paper. Minutes later Alastair's grumpy-looking face was staring up at them.

'That's him all right,' Rajiv said, taking the sketch. 'Thanks, Nimal. We'll keep you posted, Jack.'

Rajiv left some of his team at the office, in case any calls came through from the kidnappers. Jack and Helen shooed everyone off to bed telling them to get some rest, even if they could not sleep.

CHAPTER 17

Pyromaniacs

In the meantime, what *had* happened to the younger girls? The assumptions made by Rohan and the others were correct. When Alastair had asked them to deliver something to Helen's friends, the girls, not suspecting anything unusual, had gone to deliver the packages. Since Bhopinder was busy, they had not interrupted him. Waving to the man from the catering service, they rounded the corner and found the blue car. Going up to it the girls opened their courier bags to give the packages to the man who got out to meet them. Before they knew what he was about, he had grabbed them both – and seconds later Don and George jumped out of the car and helped shove the girls in. Don got into the front seat and the childproof locks were activated so that the girls could not escape.

George got in the back with the girls. The driver, whom the girls now recognized as Eugene from the campaign, started the car while Don fastened his seat belt. Just then, Gina pulled off her hair clip and, quickly rolling down the window, threw it out.

'Hey,' yelled George, leaning over to roll up the window again. 'What do you think you're doing? Eugene, lock the windows, too. This brat threw something out – should we stop and find it?'

'No time,' muttered Eugene, 'just control those kids.' He was checking to see that no one saw them driving out of the parking lot.

'If you two don't behave,' snarled Don, turning round from the front seat and shaking his fist at them, 'I'll whack you!'

The girls cringed in their seats, holding hands for comfort.

'Don't touch them, Don!' said Eugene sharply.

''Okay, okay,' mumbled Don sulkily, 'but these brats really bug me.'

'Then you shouldn't have come,' snapped Eugene, edgily. 'Now, shut your face!'

After travelling for over an hour, they reached a deserted spot near the sea where a motor boat was moored. Eugene stopped the car and told the girls to get out.

'Now, if you don't struggle and make a noise, you won't get hurt,' he said, producing two large scarves. The girls were blindfolded, carried into the boat and placed on the floor. The boat started up and sped away.

Half an hour later, the boat slowed down and came to a stop. There was no sound to be heard, other than the murmuring of waves and the cry of seagulls. The children were carried out of the boat and onto what felt, by the way it rocked, like another boat. They were led down some stairs and into a cabin. Their blindfolds were removed but they could not see outside as all the windows were blackened.

'There's plenty of food and drink, so you won't starve,' said Eugene, 'and there's a bed with blankets and sheets in the next cabin with a little bathroom next to it. There's no use shouting – no one will hear you. We're on a lonely island, far away from the Conservation. We'll check up on you tomorrow morning.'

Eugene and the boys left, locking the door behind them.

Gina immediately ran to the next cabin, but those windows were blackened, too. Mich looked as if she might cry at any moment, but Gina went over and gave her a hug.

'Don't worry, Mich,' said the little girl bravely. 'I know the others will find us soon. Come on, I'm hungry. Let's have something to eat, and then think about what we can do.'

Encouraged by Gina's chatter, Mich pulled herself together. Nothing like this had ever happened to her before, and she was frightened, but seeing the way Gina handled things, she wanted to be brave like her friend. The girls managed to have a good meal and then lay down on the bed to talk things over.

However, tired out from all their courier work, they soon fell asleep, cuddled up close together like two little puppies, the gentle rocking of the boat soothing them.

They slept through the night, and the next morning, Gina woke up with a jerk as the boat rocked violently. 'Where am I?' she mumbled, looking around at the unfamiliar room. Then the events of the previous evening came flooding back, and she lay down again so as not to disturb Mich who was still fast asleep.

'What woke me up?' said Gina to herself. 'It sounded like a whistle, but . . . the boat rocked like crazy. I can still feel big waves slapping against it.' She lay thinking about what the others would be doing and how worried they must be.

'Gina?' muttered Mich, a while later, sitting up in bed and remembering where they were. 'Do you think Uncle Jack and the others will find us today?'

'I hope so,' said Gina, getting out of bed. 'Gosh, it's nearly ten – let's eat something before those nasties return. They take away my appetite!'

Laughing, despite their imprisonment, the girls ate a hearty meal; Mich even fried sausages on the little stove in a corner of the cabin.

'Too bad we can't escape,' said Gina.

Time crawled by. Around three, they heard the sound of a motor boat; then male voices and footsteps echoed above deck, and the door opened. Alastair entered, followed by Eugene, and smiled nastily at the girls.

'It *was* you! Rohan and Nimal were right about you being a bad man,' said Gina angrily, glaring at Alastair.

'Enough from you, brat,' growled Alastair. 'None of your lip.'

Gina fell silent while the men stocked up more cans of food and put perishables in the fridge. Then they went off, not bothering to say anything more to the youngsters.

The girls breathed a sigh of relief. Unpleasant though it was to be locked in the cabin, it was worse when the men were there.

'Shh! I don't think they've gone,' whispered Mich, 'I can hear their voices somewhere.'

They listened carefully, trying to figure out where the men were. Mich went into the bedroom and climbed onto the bed. Excitedly she signalled Gina to join her. Voices were coming through a crack in the boards – the men were obviously up on the deck.

'I don't know where we can find a hideout for ourselves,' said Eugene anxiously. 'The police are all over the place. I got a call from Ingram, telling us to keep out of sight, and to make sure the boys are unavailable, too.'

'Well, they're okay on the other boat – and there's enough room for us, too,' said Alastair grumpily. 'We'll just tow it over next to this one, and no one will suspect we're hiding out in a couple of derelict boats. I don't see what all the fuss is about; Larkin will cough up the dough. In any case, we can't be traced back to Ingram. You and the boys are supposed to be in England and nobody knows I work for him.'

'They've already traced you back to Ingram,' said Eugene caustically. 'You made such a "pleasant" volunteer that you're a prime suspect. The police got hold of Ingram's payroll records and found your name on them.'

'Oh, dry up,' snarled Alastair, moodily kicking a seat. 'They won't find me. We'll get out of it one way or another, like we did the last time.'

'Only just,' muttered Eugene. 'Okay – let's get off this wreck and get the boys to help us lug the other one over. Too bad it's miles away – it'll take us hours to get back.'

'Well, as long as we're back by this evening and can check on those flags, it doesn't matter,' said Alastair.

The sound of their voices faded and, a few minutes later, the girls heard a motor boat start up and speed away.

'Now what?' asked Mich, flopping down onto the bed. 'If we're so far away from the Conservation and nobody knows where we are, how can they even start looking for us? And what flags are they talking about?'

'I don't know,' said Gina. 'But let's see if we can escape before the men come back. This boat's ancient and quite cracked in places – shall we try and make a hole in a weak spot?'

She looked up at the ceiling and her eyes lit up as she saw the crack through which the voices had filtered. 'We'll start here,' she said, standing up on the bed. 'Oh, if only we had a bar or something with which to make this hole bigger.'

'I saw a hammer in a corner of the cupboard where they put the food – let's use that,' said Mich excitedly, rushing off and returning with the implement.

'Great,' said Gina.

Working strenuously, they hammered at the weak spot and pulled at the deteriorating wood, till they had made a large gap in the roof.

'Phew,' panted Gina, collapsing on the bed to catch her breath, 'I think that's big enough.'

'Sure is,' said Mich with a gasp. 'Come on – let's get out of this dump.'

'Hang on,' said Gina. 'I'm hungry, and who knows how long we'll have to wait before we get food. Let's pack some stuff in our knapsacks.'

'Good idea,' said Mich. 'I'm starving, too.'

They packed some food, and strapped their knapsacks onto their backs. Then, placing a chair on the bed to give them a boost to the ceiling, the two little gymnasts quickly climbed out and found themselves on the deck of the boat. They were facing the land and could see several other ancient boats which were moored to rotting piers. They were just about to walk off the boat, when Gina stopped suddenly.

'Let's just go to the other end for a second – if there are any boats we could get a ride back,' she said.

'Okay,' said Mich.

They picked their way across the boat, stumbling over rusted iron hooks, broken equipment and ropes, till they were facing the sea.

'Look!' exclaimed Gina, 'We're quite close to another island, Mich – not in the middle of nowhere, like those guys said.'

'You know what?' said Mich, gazing at the land across from them. 'Those men were bluffing . . . I think we're opposite our Conservation – look at those arms like a bay – isn't that Dolphin Bay?'

'Gosh, you're right, Mich,' said Gina. 'Wait, I have binocs in my knapsack.'

She fished out the binoculars and the girls looked through them in turn. Sure enough, they could see the tiered seating on the arms of the bay. Further on, they could even see the wall for the sky-train.

'If we're this close,' said Gina thoughtfully, sitting down on a pile of rope, 'there must be a way we can get across.'

'It's too far to swim,' said Mich.

'But . . . if we had help,' said Gina, her eyes lighting up, 'we could easily do it! I know – the dolphins!'

'But . . . but . . . do they come this way?' stammered Mich.

'This morning a whistling sound woke me, and I couldn't imagine what it was,' said Gina. 'I'm sure it was the dolphins – you know the way they whistle to each other and make those clicking sounds. Also, something rocked the boat – I thought they were just waves – but it could have been the dolphins. Look, it's nearly 4:45, and in fifteen minutes they'll be coming to play with the DPs. Let's try and call them – they'll know us for sure.'

The little girls waited impatiently, looking in the direction where they knew the dolphins would soon appear. Sure enough, at 5 o'clock they saw the heptad zooming along, leaping and playing in the water as they swam towards the bay. Unfortunately, just then, a number of tourist motor boats also went past with a roar, blocking their view of the heptad. The girls yelled and waved madly to the boats, hoping somebody would see them, but the people on it were too busy looking at the dolphins.

'I guess they didn't hear us,' said Gina hoarsely, slumping down on the ropes. The dolphins had disappeared into the bay. 'Just our luck that those motor boats went past at the same time.'

'And now we're stuck,' said Mich miserably, dropping down beside her. 'What next? I guess we should hide before those men come back.'

'Yeah, we should,' said Gina, immediately picking herself up and squaring her shoulders. 'Let's find a good hiding place close by. Wish we could attract the attention of the DPs when they come to the bay to play with the dolphins.'

'Can't we tie a sheet to a pole or something?' asked Mich. 'They'd see that, wouldn't they?'

'Not obvious enough,' said Gina.

'What about a fire, then?' said Mich.

Gina gazed at her in silence for a second and then, letting out a shriek of joy, gave her an enormous hug.

'Genius! Whizz-kid, Mich!' yelled Gina, running back to the hole they had made and slipping inside the cabin once more, Mich at her heels.

'We need some paper, matches and oil from the stove, and we're all set – we'll set this boat on fire!' said Gina, picking up the items as she spoke and handing some to Mich.

'What! I meant a bonfire – not the boat!' gasped Mich, looking at her wide-eyed. 'Won't we get into awful trouble?'

'I doubt it,' said Gina, merrily, as she and Mich took the things and climbed up on deck again. 'This is a piece of junk, and I'm sure no one will care because it must belong to the crooks. Come on – help me pour this oil all over the deck and spread the paper around. Isn't it fun being pyromaniacs?'

Working quickly, the girls got things ready to start a fire. Gina struck a match to a piece of paper and threw the paper into the middle of the deck where she had poured oil over some dry rope. It caught fire immediately.

The girls jumped off the boat and watched the fire spread rapidly – the wood was rotten and dry, for the most part, and the oil certainly helped. Soon the heat was too strong for the girls to stay close to the boat, so they moved some distance away and hid in a thick bush near the water's edge.

CHAPTER 18

The Heptad to the Rescue

Back at the Centre, none of the adults got much sleep. Due to sheer exhaustion, the teens managed a few hours and met over a late breakfast, feeling dispirited. Jack and Mike were nowhere to be seen.

'The trouble is Australia's so vast,' groaned Amy. 'They could be anywhere.'

'Yeah – and it's extremely frustrating to sit around and wait,' growled Nimal.

'Why don't you visit the dolphins?' suggested Aunty Meg, when they joined her in Helen's office.

But none of them wanted to be far from the office.

Rajiv, Jack and Mike called to update everyone on what had been accomplished.

'To summarize,' said Rajiv, over the speakerphone, 'we know Ingram's involved, though he won't admit it, and we have no proof. Two of his men, Alastair and Eugene, can't be located. Neither can Don and George. Ingram told us that Eugene and the boys were in the UK, but they haven't left the country – we've checked the airports. We're checking cars, too – so far, no luck. We'll comb the sea and all the little islands today; it's possible they ditched the car and took to the water, but I believe they're close by. We've temporarily confiscated Ingram's seaplane. The news media is making announcements every fifteen minutes and we'll send helicopters out over the sea.'

'Well, I guess I'd better organize the money for those ruffians,' said Jack.

'Uncle Jack, I have an idea,' said Rohan hesitantly. The boy had been unusually silent as he mulled things over.

'Go ahead, son,' said Jack.

'Okay – I agree with Rajiv that the thugs must be fairly close. Since they want us to post white flags around Dolphin Bay it means that they can see the bay from wherever they are. Also, as Rajiv said, they're probably somewhere on the water. So, if we post the flags, they'll think we've given in to their demands and I'm positive they'll check for flags around six or earlier. Everyone should be on the alert for anything suspicious at that time.'

'And we could go out in the motor boat and use our binoculars to look for anything unusual and inform the police, so they can check it out,' said Anu.

'Good thinking, folks,' said Rajiv. 'I'll make arrangements immediately. Don't bother with the money, Jack. I think we're going to find those girls soon – unharmed.'

'Okay, then, we'll see you this evening,' said Jack, and they rang off.

'Right,' said Rohan to Helen, 'let's do the flags.'

They made fifteen flags.

'Let's take our swimming gear,' said Rohan, as they picked up their binoculars from the tents. 'It's nearly four – the dolphins will arrive at five, and I'm sure none of us will be able to resist playing with them.'

'Great, yaar,' said Nimal, smiling for the first time that day. 'Come on, Hunter – we're going to see Billy and the others.'

Hunter wagged his tail and perked up his ears, whining softly. He had been feeling gloomy, too, because he could not find the little girls, and he knew that the others were worried.

The teens and Hunter arrived at the bay to find only Ian there – the other DPs were still sick.

'We've brought the flags, Ian,' said Anu. 'We'll put them up and then go out in the boat to scout around.'

'Good idea,' said Ian. 'Since I have to run a few errands, I'll leave you to greet and play with the heptad. Good luck.'

After helping them to put up the flags, Ian went off to check on the DPs. Five minutes later, the dolphins danced into the bay.

The children went to meet them and their spirits were uplifted by the smiling faces of the dolphins, especially by Billy's funny tricks and games with Hunter.

'Oh, I wish I could keep you forever,' said Amy, hugging Rosie who was begging for cuddles.

'Look at Benji,' said Rohan suddenly.

The dolphin had zoomed to the entrance of the bay and was standing on his tail fin, whistling loudly to the other dolphins. The dolphins sped across the bay to join Benji and stood on their tail fins, too –

whistling and clicking rapidly. Then Billy came rushing back to the watching teens. He nudged Nimal and then swam back to join Benji.

'Something's up,' said Nimal, diving into the water and swimming across the bay, the others following quickly, while Hunter raced around on land to join them.

They reached the arms of the bay, clambered out of the water and looked around. The dolphins had disappeared.

'Where have they gone?' said Anu in surprise.

'There!' said Amy, pointing straight ahead as the dolphins leapt out of the water. 'And look, there's a fire! Call the fire brigade quickly!'

'All the mobiles are in the pavilion,' groaned Rohan.

'I'm sure the dolphins know that someone needs help,' said Nimal 'and that's where they're going.'

'Quick,' said Rohan, 'into the boat.'

They tumbled in, Rohan started the boat, and they headed towards the fire.

Soon they could see the dolphins swimming cautiously around a blazing boat.

'There's no sign of anyone on the boat,' said Amy. 'Good! Perhaps no one's in danger – it looks like a piece of junk.'

'How could it catch fire just like that?' said Rohan. 'There are several other derelict boats and none of them are burning.'

He moored the motor boat at an old pier.

'Watch out for rotting wood,' he called.

Stepping gingerly across the pier, the teens moved towards the burning boat.

'Hey – look at these footprints,' said Rohan suddenly, bending down near the boat. 'They're small and quite fresh. I wonder . . .'

Just then, Hunter barked! Excitedly he darted around the boat, nose to the ground; 100 metres away, he stopped at another ancient boat, sniffed again and then jumped into it.

Rohan followed him down the narrow steps to the cabin door and tried to open it – it was locked. Hunter leapt up at the door, whining, so Rohan kicked it open and peered into the single room. Two scared faces gazed up at him from a corner.

'Rohan!' shrieked Gina, jumping up and flinging herself at her brother, who caught her in a bear hug.

Mich flung herself at him, too, and the boy hugged them both in relief, and carried them out of the boat.

What laughter and joy there was at the reunion!

'We set fire to the boat in which they locked us up. But then we heard a motor boat and thought it was them coming back, so we ran and hid!' chorused the youngsters.

'I'm so glad you're safe, chickens,' said Amy, tears of relief pouring down her face, as she and Anu tried to hug both girls at once.

'And aren't you brave,' said Anu, 'setting fire to that boat. Come on – let's go back and tell Uncle Jack, before he thinks we've been kidnapped, too.'

'Not so fast!' growled a rough voice.

The JEACs gasped in dismay and turned to find Alastair, Eugene, Don and George standing behind them, guns at the ready.

'Come on – move it!' snarled Alastair. 'Over there – all of you – now!'

Another motor boat was moored next to theirs.

Hunter, hearing strange voices, came rushing out of the cabin, growling menacingly. Alastair raised his gun and warned the children to keep him under control unless they wanted him shot. Nimal grabbed Hunter's collar and hung on.

Chivvied along by the thugs, the youngsters climbed into the boat, along with Hunter – Alastair knew they would be more acquiescent if he threatened their dog. The JEACs were made to sit on the floor, Nimal holding on to Hunter, while Alastair, Don and George sat on a bench and trained their guns on them. Eugene freed the boat from its moorings and took the wheel, but before he could start her up, the boat lurched as something heavy struck it.

'Hey!' he exclaimed, letting go of the wheel as he lost his balance. The boat rocked violently. He tried to rise, slipped on a patch of oil and fell, hitting his head against the wheel. He was out for the count!

The other crooks were trying to maintain their balance, and as the boat lurched again, George's gun flew out of his hands – into the sea. As everyone tried to stand up and hang on to something, a huge dolphin leapt out of the water, across the front of the boat, whistling and clicking loudly.

'It's Benji and the rest of the heptad!' yelled Nimal, seeing the other dolphins butting against the boat. 'Come on, heptad – to the rescue!'

'Put a bullet in them,' roared Don, struggling to keep his balance.

'Don't you dare!' shouted Amy, who was standing next to him. She grabbed his gun, Anu joining her, and they struggled to get it from him. He tried to hit them, but Rohan, holding on to the side of the boat, managed to kick the gun out of his hands. With another kick he floored Don and stood over him threateningly.

Nimal aimed a karate kick at Alastair who dropped his gun and was promptly bitten by Hunter. The man screamed in pain, leaning against the side of the boat. Nimal bent down quickly, grabbed him around the knees and heaved. With a loud yell, Alastair fell into the sea.

'Helllppp! I'm drowning! I can't swim!' howled Alastair, as his head rose above the water.

'Oh, for crying out aloud!' exclaimed Nimal, and dove into the ocean. He grabbed Alastair and brought him to the edge of the boat, where the girls pulled him in – he was quite subdued. George, who had given up quickly, was pushed over beside Alastair, and Hunter stood guard over them.

Nimal leaned over the side of the boat, whistling and clicking softly to the dolphins. They immediately understood that their friends were safe and stopped rocking the boat – but they didn't leave.

'Let's tie up these chaps,' said Rohan. 'Amy, Anu – find some rope.'

Soon, the four ruffians – including Eugene, who was sitting up groggily – were securely tied. They were all subdued.

'Look, Eugene's got a mobile,' said Rohan. 'Let's call Uncle Jack and tell him the girls are safe and we've caught the crooks. The police will be at the Conservation, too, and they can pick up this nice bunch of flowers! I'll take us back.'

'Why don't you do the honours, Amy,' said Nimal with a grin, handing Eugene's mobile to her.

She quickly dialled the number.

'Uncle Jack, it's Amy. Where are you? Great – and is Rajiv with you, too? Good! We've got news – the girls are safe with us – whoa!' Amy held the phone away from her ear and the others heard Jack's shout of joy. 'We've also caught the crooks and are on the way back to Dolphin Bay. What's that? Super – oh, and by the way, please have tons of fish for the dolphins – they saved our lives. Bye for now.'

She rang off and turned to the others with a broad smile on her face. 'Uncle Jack, Rajiv and Mike are all at the Conservation, and are running down to the bay!'

'Let's go, Rohan,' said Anu.

Rohan started the boat and they sped towards Dolphin Bay, escorted by the dolphins, frolicking in the water beside them or racing ahead of the boat.

As they neared the bay they saw a large crowd in the pavilion. Monique had made the joyful announcement over the PA system. More staff members came rushing in as the JEACs arrived with their captured cargo.

Rohan took the boat right into the bay, and the JEACs and Hunter tumbled out into the shallow water. Everyone was there, including the sick DPs. Jack, Mike, Monique and Helen waded into the water to hug the little girls. Jack would not let go of them but insisted on carrying them before handing them over to waiting arms. Then he went back into the water with a large barrel of fish and fed the dolphins as he stroked and hugged each of them, too.

The dolphins, ecstatic with joy, were whistling and clicking merrily, their smiley faces showing how much they loved the fish and all the attention. Billy, the comic, took five fish in his mouth and tried to feed Hunter, who was also splashing about in the water.

Everybody wanted to know what had happened, and the villains got many dirty looks. However, Jack announced that they could hear the story at dinner, in an hour and a half, and the crowd dispersed slowly. The policemen took the troublemakers to the police station; Jack and Rajiv would go down later on to decide what action should be taken against them.

Saying goodbye to the dolphins and thanking them once again with hugs and cuddles for rescuing them, the JEACs went back to shower and change. Ian would escort the dolphins outside the bay and join the rest of the Conservation staff for dinner.

Given that they did not have much time in which to prepare a feast, the culinary team had done a marvellous job! Appetizing scents wafted around the room and the tables groaned under their load of delicious food. Extra chairs had been brought in and, though the tables were crowded, no one minded the crush.

As everyone settled down with a plate of food, Jack invited Anu, known for her storytelling skills, to narrate the complete story, starting from the plane trip where they had overheard Ingram and Owen talking. As usual, Anu involved the other JEACs. People heard, for the first time, what had happened to Gina and Mich; Gina, in a good imitation of her sister, drew Mich out of her shyness and made her tell part of the story.

Anu concluded by saying that if not for the dolphins, they would have been in even more trouble, and everybody agreed with her.

It was an exhausted group of people who dispersed, shortly after dinner, and went straight to bed. Jack insisted that everyone sleep in the next day, and that work could start once they were well rested.

The children said goodnight and left the dining room, Rohan and Nimal insisting on carrying the two little girls on their shoulders, 'just in case someone else tries to kidnap you,' said Rohan with a smile. Anu and Amy led the way to the tents, carrying two jugs of hot chocolate which the staff had given them before they left the food hall.

Seated in the girls' tents, the little girls already in their sleeping bags, the JEACs sipped their hot chocolate contentedly.

'It's *so* good to have both of you back, safe and sound,' said Anu, gently tugging one of Gina's curls. 'I must say, you've been very brave.'

'Yeah, for sure! But what impresses me most,' said Rohan gravely, looking at the two sleepy little faces, 'is the way you both kept your heads and managed, not only to escape, but also to attract attention so that you could be rescued.'

The others agreed, and after hugs – and licks by Hunter – the boys went to their own tent. Soon there was nothing but deep breathing to be heard.

CHAPTER 19

Everything Comes Together

After a refreshing sleep, everyone went back to work with extra vigour. Only one week remained to Opening Day – and there was lots to be done. There were shows to be practised, finishing touches to be given to the whole area, Christmas decorations to be put up, a bandstand to be set up for the Frolicsome Four and last-minute emergencies to be dealt with. People were calling in, accepting the invitations sent out earlier – and the list of things to do appeared to be a never-ending one!

The JEACs had tons of work and were getting excited because all their parents would be able to make it to the Opening Day.

'I'm so glad that we'll not only meet one another's parents, but that they'll also meet each other,' said Amy.

She and the other girls were being fitted in the dressmaker's chalet and had to try on the various outfits for the shows they were participating in.

'I know our dads have already met, Amy – at some conference or other,' said Anu, 'but our mothers haven't, and Nimal's parents haven't met yours at all.'

'These are great outfits,' said Gina, as she and Mich came out of the changing room, wearing pretty little swimsuits for their dolphin show.

'You look like circus girls,' said Anu with a smile.

'The sequins are lovely,' said Amy, admiring the girls.

After they'd finished with the dressmaker, they joined the men and boys for lunch. They had not seen Jack and Mike since the previous night and were eager for news.

'What happened at the police station, Uncle Jack?' asked Rohan, as soon as everyone was seated.

'Well, Rajiv and his team of interrogators pulled all the information we needed out of Eugene, Don and George,' said Jack. 'Alastair, though – he was a real tough nut to crack. However, we have enough incriminating evidence to put them in jail, including John Ingram and Darrel Owen. Rajiv arrested both Ingram and Owen last night.'

'Good,' growled Nimal, 'and for how long will they all be in jail?'

Jack didn't answer and Mike, with a wry grin, said, 'Well, you know Jack and his soft heart. He felt that it wouldn't be constructive if the two boys were jailed – so they're being sent to a correctional institution for teenage delinquents. But if they ever participate in any other criminal activities, they will go to jail.'

'I know they were perfectly horrible, Uncle Jack,' said Anu, 'but I guess you've done what you and Dad always tell us to do – tempered justice with mercy – and I hope those boys appreciate it.'

'Thank you, love,' said Jack, giving her a warm look. 'I had to control my "temper" quite a bit before I could be "merciful".'

'As for the men,' continued Mike, 'they are going jail for a minimum of ten years. Since Ingram has lots of money, it's possible that their lawyers will manage to get Ingram and Owen a shorter sentence, since they both insist they had no idea that the others had planned to kidnap the girls. But they're finished in the Gold Coast and, in fact, in Brisbane. If they do get off the hook, they'll have to relocate.'

'So that's that!' said Rohan. 'I guess it's a good thing the boys were given a milder sentence. I hope they've learned their lesson.'

'I hope so, too, Rohan,' said Jack. 'Now, let's forget about them and get ready for OD!'

Things went more or less smoothly, with the usual quota of small hitches, which people took in their stride, and soon it was only three days to OD.

The Patels – both Rohan's and Nimal's parents – arrived on the same flight, early on the morning of the nineteenth, and Hunter and the children, including Amy and Mich, went out to the airport to meet them.

The Patels were delighted to meet the Larkin girls, who were not given a chance to feel shy or left out. They were installed in Jack and Mike's chalets while the Larkins would have a room in Helen's. The youngsters wanted them to come and see all their activities and meet the dolphins, and their parents were pleased to see how they had developed their talents and how well they were learning to work together. Naturally the adults all fell in love with the dolphins, too!

In the evening, the Larkins arrived and were again met by the JEACs and others. A wonderful reunion of friends, old and new, took place. The Larkins were charmed to meet the Patels, of whom they had heard so much, and Hunter brought all the women flowers, which impressed everyone and earned him extra pats and treats.

'I can't believe how talkative Mich is,' said Janet Larkin to Dilki and Jo Patel, as they chatted over an after dinner coffee. 'She's normally so shy – your four have done wonders for her.'

'They're certainly not shy,' laughed Dilki, 'but I notice that Gina is more confident, too. It's good for her to have a friend her own age.'

'They're a great group of kids,' said Jack, as he and Jim Patel joined the ladies, 'and I think we should give them more opportunities to spend time together. They learn from and support each other incredibly well. I know they live continents apart – but perhaps on holidays?'

'Couldn't agree more,' said Jim Patel. 'In fact, next . . . but here comes the mob. I'll tell you about it later, once things are confirmed.'

CHAPTER 20

Opening Day!

At last it was Opening Day.

People came from all over Australia and from many other parts of the world, too. Eager conservationists, volunteers, families, friends, government officials – you name them, they were there!

The Prime Minister of Australia was the guest of honour, and at 10:30 a.m. Jack welcomed everybody, the Prime Minister made a short speech, and his wife cut the ribbons which stretched across the gates. He and his wife entered the Centre first, Jack and Mike escorting them. The others were then allowed to enter, in families or groups of ten, so that they could be welcomed by the volunteers and some of the staff, and also so that statistics could be taken of the number of people at the OD. The entrance fee on Opening Day was only two dollars per head, but anyone who wished to, could make a donation as they left. Fundraising volunteers were at the gates to give each adult or family a form to fill out with their name, address and telephone number, so that they could be sent a tax deductible receipt. The car parks were chock-a-block – and the police had to ask people to park their cars along the sides of the roads.

It was a wonderful day! The shows were a roaring success, the sky-train went round the track non-stop, the Frolicsome Four were a hit, and there was brisk business at the souvenir shops, restaurants, coffee and juice booths. People were in a good humour and ready to appreciate everything. The dolphins and the seals were heart stealers, and folks wanted to attend all the shows to watch these fascinating creatures. Ultimately, Jack appealed to their generosity and sense of fair play by asking that everyone be given the opportunity to watch the shows. The children, on seeing Nimal, Gina, Mich and Hunter play with the dolphins, clamoured to be allowed to play with them, too, but parents had been warned to keep an eye on their children, and no accidents occurred.

All too soon it was 6 p.m. and people started leaving. Not one person failed to make a donation at the gate on their way out – they had had such a marvellous time and knew that it was well worth supporting such a fantastic cause. Some of them were coming back, later that evening, for the more formal fundraising gala dinner, and many of the corporate donors who were unable to attend during the day would attend this event.

The children rushed off to dress. Their parents had brought out suits for the boys and party dresses for the girls, and Mrs. Patel had even remembered to bring a nice red bow tie for Hunter, which he wore proudly.

The pavilion and the lawns on one side of the lake, close to the food hall, had been lit with a myriad fairy lights, all twinkling brilliantly. Beautifully decorated tables were set out and an orchestra was playing softly. Two thousand guests were expected and they started arriving around 8 p.m. There were a hundred waiters and waitresses, dressed in black and white uniforms, circulating among the guests – all volunteers from the nearby Hotel School – and the Maitre D' was resplendent in his tails!

The JEACs wandered around, talking to the staff and volunteers they had befriended, and meeting up with James from the Glenforest Sanctuary and Ralph, their tour guide. They ended up at their table, next to the one where their parents were seated with Jack, Mike, Helen, Monique, the Prime Minister and his wife, and a few others they did not know.

The culinary staff of the Conservation had prepared a feast which 'made the gastronomic juices flow like a river', as Nimal put it hungrily. It was a superb evening.

The fundraiser was a huge success and raised over two million dollars that evening – exclusive of the donations made earlier in the day. Jack, as he made the announcement from the pavilion, asked everyone to raise their glasses as he toasted the Conservation Centre, the staff, the volunteers, the guests, the JEACs and, of course, the Dolphin Heptad, without whom this event could not have taken place! The Prime Minister and his wife left around midnight – after insisting that they shake hands with the JEACs – and encouraged the youngsters to enroll more youth in their group. Others drifted off gradually.

After the Prime Minister's departure, Jim Patel came over to the table where the JEACs were seated, bringing with him a young couple.

'Folks, I'd like you to meet Mr. and Mrs. Vijaydasa from Sri Lanka. Lalith, Priyani – these are the Larkin and Patel offspring, commonly known as the JEACs!'

The youngsters stood up to shake hands with the Vijaydasas, introducing themselves and Hunter.

'Lalith and Priyani manage the Alighasa Wildlife Conservation Centre in Walapitiya, in the heart of Sri Lanka,' continued Mr. Patel. 'I'm going back with them in the New Year to visit their Conservation, and your dad's coming with me, Nimal – he's going to write some special computer programs for them.'

'Wow – that's neat,' said Nimal. 'Does the Centre have any endangered species, Mr. Vijaydasa?'

'Why, yes,' said Mr. Vijaydasa, 'and please call us Lalith and Priyani – we focus on elephants and strive to protect them from irate farmers and also from people who want to shoot the males for their ivory.'

'That's terrible,' said Amy. 'In *Planet Zoo*, author Simon Barnes says that the Asian elephant is in grave danger because of deforestation.'

'Unfortunately, that's true, too,' said Priyani in her soft voice. 'However, we have a growing group of conservationists in Sri Lanka, and we're slowly creating awareness in the country.'

'We were wondering,' continued Lalith, winking at Jim, 'if you children had any definite plans for next summer?'

'No, not yet. Why?' asked Rohan.

'Well, we would like to invite all of you to join us in Sri Lanka, in July – if you'd like to,' said Lalith.

'Yippee! Another great trip! Hurrah!' yelled the JEACs – and then stopped in embarrassment as the adults laughed.

'We would love that – really – and thank you so much for inviting us,' said Rohan, hurriedly remembering his manners.

The others joined in, thanking the Vijaydasas for their kind invitation.

'Well, your parents said you were very good at fundraising, and perhaps you could start off a Sri Lankan branch of JEACs,' said Priyani with a laugh. 'So you may have another working holiday. Hope that's okay with all of you.'

'Another busman's holiday would suit me just fine,' said Gina formally, her eyes glowing with excitement. 'I love ephalunts – especially the baby ones.'

'I've only seen them in zoos,' said Mich eagerly. 'Can we ride them?'

'Of course you can,' laughed Lalith, 'and give them a bath, too!'

Jack and the other Larkins, the Patels, Mike, Monique, Helen and many of the staff the children had worked with, came up to join them.

Then Jack stood on a chair and raised his glass. 'Ladies, gentlemen, JEACs and Hunter – a toast to all of you! Thank you for your hard work, support and encouragement, and for making this Opening Day a roaring success. Also, a special thank you to the JEACs! If not for your dedication to the projects we set you, and courage in the face of danger, we may not have been able to open this Conservation today.'

Everybody raised their glasses and roared out, 'Cheers, JEACs! Well done! And cheers to all of us, too!'

The children felt a warm glow of happiness.

Life was great! Life was superfantabulous! They had yet another holiday to look forward to – in another country – making new friends with both animals and humans. And the nicest part of it all was that the Patels and the Larkins would see one another again in six months. Could anyone ask for more? Not the JEACs!

Perhaps just one more thing – *how about another adventure?*

*   *   *

GLOSSARY

Word	Meaning
Ad	Advertisement – short form
AFC&DB	Aquatic Fantasia Conservation and Dolphin Bay – acronym
APs	Aged Parents – acronym
Aunty/aunties	Nimal uses it on the girls in mock respect
Aussie	Australia or Australian – informal
Binocs	Binoculars – short form
Biscuits	Cookies
Boot (of a cab/car)	The trunk of a cab/car
Brekker	Breakfast – short form
Brill	Brilliant – short form
Brunch	A late morning meal eaten instead of breakfast and lunch
Canuck	Canadian – informal
Deep Heat	A topical heat rub manufactured by Mentholatum to relieve muscle sprains
Dekko	Look – Hindi
Dope	A drug taken illegally
DPs	Dolphin Playmates – acronym
Egg bhujia	Scrambled eggs with onion, tomato and green chillies
Ephalunt	Elephant – fun usage of word
Exactimo	Exactly – fun usage of word
Fab	Fabulous – short form
G'day, G'dai	Good day
GK	General Knowledge – acronym
Goodonya	Good on you; well done; good for you!
Heffalump	A child's term for an elephant (coined by A.A. Milne in *Winnie-the-Pooh*)
Heptad	A group of seven
Hols	Holidays – short form (vacation)
Hon	Honey – short form
Khidr	Where – Hindi
Lift	Elevator
Maite	Mate, said with a pronounced accent
Maître D'	Head waiter of a restaurant or manager of a hotel
Mes amis	My friends – French
Moi	Me – French

Word	Meaning
Nineteen to the dozen	Talks a lot – idiom
No problemo	No problem – fun usage of word
Owyagoin'	How are you going? How are you?
Oxford	A prestigious university in England
PA system	Abbreviation for public address system: a system of microphones, amplifiers and loudspeakers
Paraphernalia	Miscellaneous articles, especially the equipment needed for a particular activity
Pavlova	A favourite Australian dessert (meringue, fruit and cream), named after the famous Russian ballerina, Anna Pavlova
PC	Politically Correct – acronym
Pax	Latin for peace; a call for a truce
Petrol	Gas
PhD	Doctor of Philosophy
Plonked	Set down heavily or carelessly
Pyromaniacs	People who love to set fire to things
Résumé	A quick recap, summary; also a curriculum vitae
Sky-train	A train track built above the ground
Sotto voce	In a quiet voice
Speakerphone	A telephone with a loudspeaker and microphone, which does not need to be held in the hand.
Touché	Acknowledgement of a clever point made by another person, often at one's expense
Urdu	One of the languages of India
Womyn	Woman, women – an exaggerated way of being politically correct when using the word
Yaar	Mate/buddy – most often used in India by males

ABOUT THE AUTHOR

Amelia Lionheart has been writing for many years and is the published author of four books for children. She has a diploma in writing from the Institute of Children's Literature, Connecticut, USA.

Amelia, who has lived and worked in several countries, believes very strongly in the conservation of wildlife and, in particular, the protection of endangered species. She is convinced that awareness of this issue, when imbued in children at an early age, is a vital step towards saving our planet.

As a member of several nature/wildlife preservation organizations, including the Durrell Wildlife Conservation Trust, she invites children and their families to become involved with local zoos and conservation centres and to support their important work, both by creating awareness and fundraising. To encourage this, she created a group called the Junior Environmentalists and Conservationists (JEACs) in the first book of her JEACs' series, *Peacock Feathers*. In the other books, the JEACs travel to various countries, having adventures while enlarging their group and encouraging local children to start groups of JEACs in their own countries. As of November 2013, Amelia has four *real* groups of JEACs in Canada. The JEACs continue to evolve.

Amelia's other interests include environmental issues, volunteer work and fundraising. She believes that if people from different countries explore the diversity of cultures and learn from one another, they will discover that they have more similarities than dissimilarities. Many of these ideas are included in her books.

Please check out http://www.jeacs.com, Amelia's website for children.